Forecast of Evil

~A Jenkins & Burns Mystery~

To Sharon,
Happy Reading!
Laura Bradford

Laura Bradford

HILLIARD HARRIS

HILLIARD HARRIS

P.O. Box 275
Boonsboro, Maryland 21713-0275

First Edition-June 2006
ISBN 1-59133-150-1

Book Design: S. A. Reilly
Cover Illustration © S. A. Reilly
Manufactured/Printed in the United States of America
2006

To my friend, Heather

For proving the adage that all good things—including *true* friendship—come to those who wait.

Thank you.

Acknowledgements:

Although writing is largely a solitary endeavor, many people contributed to the completion of this story in one way or another.

*My family. For understanding my need to slip into a world that is all my own. A world with characters I talk to for months, yet they've never met.

*My Saturday morning buddies: Michelle Thouviner, Vicki Berger Erwin, and Shirley Kennett. For being the kind of friends who "get" what it's all about and gladly jump right in when the conversation turns to murder plots.

*The folks at Borders Bookstore in St. Peters, Missouri. For allowing me to adopt their café—and a specific table—as my second home during the writing of this book.

*My editor, Shawn Reilly. For believing in me as a writer.

Prologue
Thursday, January 27th
11:00 a.m.

PETE GARNER STUDIED the faces of the dozen or so men standing around in thick winter coats, waiting—like he was—for Dan to get started. For them, the waiting was as much a part of the game as the game itself. It was the time when good-natured barbs were exchanged, snide comments about alcohol rampant. But for Pete, it was an extra chance to go over his strategy, memorize his route. Only this time, he was ready, route planned, confidence high, eyes focused on the prize.

"Although most of you idiots know the drill already, I thought I'd listen to the sound of my voice again and go over the rules with everybody one more time," Dan Friar said as he zipped up his thermal parka and secured his hood around his neck. "When you hear me fire the starter pistol it's every man for himself. The first one back at this spot with all ten points is our winner."

"C'mon, Dan, enough already," shouted a voice toward the back of the group. "You've got a bigger mouth than my wife, and I never thought *anyone* could steal that title. Fire the damn thing so we can find our points and head back to Sophie's for some beers."

"Would you relax? I'm trying to make sure everyone's got a crack at the prize money," Dan said. "If Pete wins one more time I'm gonna be accused of favoritism or some other sort of weird attraction you guys come up with."

"That might be the case if you actually liked Pete..."

"Now, now, boys. I *like* Pete. I just wish he'd give the rest of us a chance at winning once in a while."

"Lose some weight, Dan, and then maybe you'll have a chance," quipped Josh, one of the circle of guys.

It felt good to laugh. In fact, it had occurred to Pete recently that he felt more relaxed with this group than he did with any of the guys he worked with on a daily basis. And he had his cardiologist to thank for it. Instead of sending him home with a few cholesterol pills and a follow-up appointment card, the doctor had encouraged Pete to find a hobby that would enable him to leave work behind and enjoy a little competitive exercise.

And now, three years later, he was in the best shape of his life thanks to Dan and the rest of the orienteering club.

He looked at the men he'd gotten to know over the years. Dan, Drew, Austin, Steve...all good, hardworking guys with a shared passion for the outdoors, especially when it was mixed with a healthy dose of friendly competition.

Pete rubbed his hands together and eyed the new faces that dotted the group. There were more than usual thanks to the handful of lime green flyers Dan had left around the island over the past few days. Most of the newcomers had the same playful cockiness as the club members. Except one.

The burly redhead who stood a few feet off from the rest of the group had introduced himself as Mark. But despite Pete's attempts to strike up a real conversation with the guy, he'd learned very little, other than the fact that the newcomer liked to win just as much as Pete did. And that he knew a good compass when he saw one.

But this competition was more than just being the best at something. In fact, for the first time since he joined the club, more was at stake than just bragging rights and a free beer.

"Countin' the money already, Pete?"

He turned quickly, surprised at the accuracy of the question.

Drew.

"Man, Pete, are you ever gonna remember who taught you how to play this game?"

He felt the corners of his mouth twitch, saw the mock seriousness in Drew's eyes.

"Oh, I remember. Problem is *he* ain't here this year." Pete slapped his hand on Drew's heavily padded back and laughed.

"How quickly they forget. How quickly they forget." Drew zipped his parka to the base of his neck, snapped the hood strap across his throat. "Seriously though, what were you thinking? You were a million miles away just now."

Pete shrugged and looked at the snow beside his skis. "Actually, you weren't too far from the truth. You know, about the counting stuff. I've got plans for that money. Big plans."

"Care to share?"

"I'll tell you when I win." He pulled on his gloves and snapped the strips of leather that held them tight to his wrists.

Drew's laughter filled the cold morning air. "I'd love to argue and say I'm gonna win, however, self delusion is a waste of time. But you might get an argument from Joshie Boy."

"Why's that?"

Drew shrugged. "He claims he's gonna win this one, one way or another."

"Oh really?" Pete looked across the circle at Josh, the youngest and mouthiest of the group. A head shorter than most everyone around him, Josh had a real need for attention. Trouble was, the guy was an excellent skier and if winning was based solely on speed and agility, Josh would win hands down.

Fortunately for Pete though, Joshie Boy loved to argue almost as much as he loved attention. And until he stopped arguing with the compass, first place would continue to elude the guy in all similar competitions—skiing or otherwise.

Drew uncapped his thermos and took a sip of coffee. "He says he needs the money big time. That he can't lose."

"Why?"

"You know how the guy rambles. But, from what I could decipher between curse words, his wife caught him cheating on her." Drew wiped his mouth with the back of his gloved-hand. "She's retaliating via the court system."

Pete nodded slowly, pondered Drew's words. "Well, Joshie Boy's gonna have to find another way to pay for his screw-ups. 'Cause this prize is all mine."

"I have no doubt about that one." Drew thumped Pete's back. "Hey, I'm gonna go top off my coffee before we start. Knock 'em dead, buddy."

"Oh, I intend to." Pete glanced in Josh's direction one last time, his gaze coming to rest on the younger man's aggressive stance and determined jaw.

"Ah, hell," he muttered under his breath, pulling the topographical map from his pocket. It never hurt to double check his route, although he'd stored most of the trek in his mind already. Knowing the course ahead of time was what helped shave precious seconds off his game. So many of the other guys waited until the shot-gun start to figure out where to go, stopping repeatedly to compare coordinates to their map and compass. But that thinking never made sense to Pete. Studying the lay of the land and familiarizing yourself with direction was what it was all about. If you could visualize where you were headed, it made getting there a lot easier.

He had to admit that his initial reluctance over a winter game was for naught. The rules hadn't changed. It was just the act of getting to the designated coordinates that would be different thanks to the deep snow.

Pete unfolded the map. Much of the day's course wound through thick forest—the kind of terrain that would be tough to maneuver for mediocre skiers. Throw in the potential to get disoriented in a heavily wooded area, and this competition was sure to be tough. For all of them.

"When you find a point, mark your card with the stamp that's there," Dan said, his voice cutting through Pete's thoughts. "First person back to this spot with all ten points will walk away with four thousand dollars."

He raised the pistol into the air and paused. "Oh yeah, may someone other than Pete win."

1:00 p.m.

PETE COULD ALMOST feel the one hundred dollar bills that would be in his hand in less than thirty minutes. Forty of them, crisp and new. The final money he needed to take his wife on the second honeymoon he'd been promising her for years.

He glanced down at the Arrow 30 competition compass Eileen had given him for his birthday in November. He'd been eyeing it for months, preaching its many attributes to anyone who'd listen. Eileen didn't understand a thing about two second dampening and how the needle-steadying feature could shave crucial seconds off his competitive time, yet she listened with the eagerness of someone who did. If she thought the technological upgrade was silly, she never let it show. It was important to him, so that made it important to her.

With a burst of speed, he skied through a wide field and into the next cropping of trees. His desire to do something for Eileen was all the motivation he needed to find the last two points and claim the prize money.

Squinting between the lush branches of a mammoth evergreen tree, Pete could see he was right on target thanks to his new compass. In fact, if he was right, the ninth point should be just over that hill.

He leaned his pole against a tree and pulled the map from his sleeve.

"Okay, let's see. I should be right—here." He forced his index finger to move forward along the line he'd drawn, felt its clumsiness inside his glove. The temperature was dropping. Fast.

He glanced up. The angle he'd chosen to approach the gulley had worked. It was narrow enough in this area that he'd be able to step across it easily. Then he'd just fly over the next hill and get number nine.

Pete smiled down at the map then tucked it back into his sleeve. He was so confident of his impending win that he took a moment to admire the beautiful snow-laden landscape. There was no doubt about it. Dan had outdone himself with this competition. Mackinac Island was beautiful.

Pete pushed off with his poles and skied across the sun-dappled snow, headed into the next section of trees that would bring him one step closer to surprising Eileen. The tall spruce trees created a slalom course that would have impressed many an Olympic skier and each snowy hill seemed steeper than the next, an impression he knew was caused by fatigue. The clip he was running the course was bound to take its toll. But he refused to let that happen. Not when he was this close.

He pushed over the last hill that stood between him and the ninth point, his eyes riveted on the stamp pad that hung from the branches a few feet away. Stopping, he pulled out his card and marked it with the green-colored stamp that would serve as proof of his find.

"I'm not too sure that fancy compass of yours is helping a whole lot."

He turned quickly, came face to face with the new guy, Mark.

"What was that?" Pete asked, sizing up the bulky redhead. Mark was taller than he was by a good two or three inches, which put the man at about six-foot-three. His shoulders were broad, the size of his biceps evident by the tight fit of his parka sleeves.

"It's only been two hours and I've already got eight points," the man bragged. "There's no way you're beating that."

Pete could feel the corners of his mouth spreading upward, the laugh that begged to be released.

"You'd be right, if I hadn't just found number nine!"

With a hard shove, Pete skied off in the direction of his tenth and final point. He hadn't thought it was possible, but his upcoming win had just gotten sweeter.

HE TOOK THE cap off the purple stamp and marked his card. His wife was going to be thrilled. She deserved this trip. She had devoted twenty-plus years to their children, putting her life on hold to give them the best possible advantages in life. She had been supportive of his constant career hopping, even when it required some serious belt-tightening to get by. But now it was her turn. Her turn to know just how much he loved and respected her.

Pete slid the completed point card into the front right pocket of his parka and looked around. The increasing cloud cover had brought a darkened chill to the air, the snow-encrusted tree branches creating an almost web-like feel to his surroundings. The thick forest that had seemed so beautiful only thirty minutes before was now different. Menacing. He shivered.

Feeling suddenly foolish, Pete stuck his poles into the ground. It was time to turn in his card, collect his prize money.

He smiled as he envisioned Eileen's reaction when he called. Prayed that his plans for a romantic cruise to the Caribbean would show her just how much he valued her and their marriage.

The extra money from the contest would help supplement the cash he'd been setting aside from his paychecks. With any luck, there'd be enough for her to go on a shopping spree before the trip to pick up some new vacation clothes. She deserved that. And so much more.

A twig snapped behind him and he turned.

"Oh, hey. What the h—"

Before he could finish his sentence, waves of pain crashed over him as the sharp metal knife bore into his chest again and again.

Thursday, January 27th
One
2:00 p.m.

THE PALE BLUE luggage tag sailed into the air like a child's kite, anchored to the earth by a short white string and the tweed-colored suitcase at her feet. Pushing a windblown curl from her forehead, Elise Jenkins leaned forward, peering down the empty pathway that led into a lush canopy of snow-covered evergreens.

"Shhh. Do you hear that? It sounds like it's getting closer."

She felt his arm slide around her waist, his warm breath against her temple as he spoke.

"Do you have any idea how happy you look right now, Lise?"

She tilted her head upward and grinned. It was nearly impossible to be anything but happy when she was standing next to Mitch Burns. Just his presence made her smile from ear to ear. Throw in the fact that they were finally here—together—and she'd put her demeanor a lot closer to giddy.

"If my face shows even a tenth of what I'm feeling right now, then yeah, I know how happy I must look."

His lips pressed against her forehead, lingered for a moment. "This is gonna be incredible, isn't it?"

"Ye—"

She stopped, her gaze riveted on the path once again. The distant hint of bells grew louder as two sleek, chestnut brown horses came into view, their hooves rising above the snow in perfect tandem.

"Oh, Mitch."

She stared at the muscular animals as they drew closer, their warm breath mingling with the cold afternoon air in tiny cloud-like puffs. A man dressed in a thick overcoat sat on a berth just behind the horses, a tan derby hat atop his bushy brown hair.

"Whoa there, fellas." The young man pulled back on the reins gently, the horses exhaling loudly as they slowed to a stop. "Are you Mitch Burns and Elise Jenkins?"

Mitch stepped forward. "Yes?"

"Your pilot called as you were leaving the mainland and told me you were on your way. I'm here to take you to your hotel."

Elise suddenly felt like a little girl on Christmas morning, thrilled at the sight of brightly wrapped packages, yet eager to see what was inside. The small bits and pieces she remembered from her childhood vacation to this island were happy ones. Her aunt and uncle had looked so in love on that trip, so full of plans for their future. It was *that* memory of them that she wanted to hold onto forever.

The driver jumped down from his seat and picked up their suitcases. "Hop in and we'll be on our way in just a minute. There's a couple of blankets under my seat. You might want to grab some for the drive into town. But be careful you don't burn yourselves on the warmer."

Elise happily took hold of Mitch's outstretched hand and allowed him to help her onto the sled. Her Christmas vision faded into every woman's dream of being Cinderella for a day. Prince Charming and all.

She settled onto the narrow, yet comfortable bench and reached for the lone red blanket beneath the driver's empty seat. The soft wool warmed her cold hands as she carefully unfolded the material.

The driver took his place behind the reins and turned to look at them, his brows furrowing. "You might want to grab the blue one too, it's gonna be a cold ride."

"Blue one?"

"The blue blank—" He broke off abruptly. "Ah, I'm sorry. I gave that one away a few hours ago, to a kid who was on the noon flight. I tried to give him a ride with the other guy from that plane, but he said he didn't have far to go. I gave him the blanket 'cuz his coat wasn't meant for the temps we get here."

"Don't worry about it. This red one should be fine." Elise spread the blanket across Mitch's lap and snuggled closer to him. "See, it works great."

"Good. Now let's get you folks to your hotel before that blanket cools off too much." The driver turned toward the horses and stopped. "Wait. Where to?"

"The Island Inn," she answered softly.

The young man clicked his tongue, urged the horses forward, their sleigh bells jingling once again.

"You warm enough?" Mitch asked her, his breath forming small white clouds as he spoke.

"Oh, yes."

She inhaled slowly, relishing the clean, cool air that filled her lungs. If there was any place on earth that could help her forget the terror of last summer, this was surely it. A place this remote, this breathtaking, was the kind of haven she had been craving for months.

"My name's Joe. If I can answer any questions for you during the ride, please ask."

Mitch scooted closer to her, taking her hand in his before turning his attention to the driver. "Do you live here year 'round?"

"I sure do. I can't imagine living anywhere else." The young man reached up and repositioned the cap on his bushy brown hair. "As a matter of fact, our quiet life has attracted a decent number of people over the years. Retirees, writers, artists. The kind of folks who crave beauty. And privacy."

"How big is the island?" Mitch asked.

"The perimeter road around the entire island is eight point three miles. No motorized vehicles are allowed anywhere on the island except for our one fire truck. And that ain't been used in over ten years. But in the winter we're allowed to use snow mobiles to get around."

"Is a plane the only access off during the winter?"

"This time of year, yeah. One of the ferryboat lines runs a limited schedule until about New Year's, but then we're down to the plane that brought you here. And even that's dependent on the weather."

"The pilot said we're in for quite a storm tonight." Mitch pulled the blanket higher on Elise's lap. "That could really shut this place down, huh?"

"Oh yeah. If we get even close to what they're predicting, it won't matter what kind of transportation we do or don't have. Because nothing will be running."

"What about cell phone coverage?" Mitch asked, looking around. "I don't notice any towers."

"There aren't any." Joe shifted in his seat and jostled the reins ever so gently. "If you're real lucky you might get spotty service but it's generally more trouble than it's worth."

Elise listened carefully, soaking up every word the driver spoke. "Do you ever feel isolated out here?" she asked suddenly.

"Most of us locals like the peace and quiet. We get our dose of the outside world when the fudgies come to town in the summer."

She laughed. "What's a fudgie?"

"That's what we call the uh, um, tourists." Joe's voice grew quiet, uncomfortable. "But don't get me wrong. We'd be hard pressed to survive out here if it weren't for visitors like yourselves."

"Don't worry, Joe. We're not offended. We come from a tourist town, too." She leaned her head against Mitch's shoulder and sighed happily. "But why do you call them fudgies?"

"Once you get down to Main Street, and you see all the fudge shops that exist because of the summer crowd, you'll understand."

"Oh we understand don't we, Mitch? Except where we come from, it's salt water taffy the tourists crave."

Mitch's laugh, deep and hearty, echoed through the tree-lined pathway. "Can you just imagine the guys in the department referring to our tourists as taffies?" He straightened in his seat, sucked in his chest, and deepened his voice as he spoke. "I just clocked a taffy goin' twenty over."

Instantly, Elise ducked her head into Mitch's chest, the image he created sending her into a fit of giggles, giggles that only multiplied as she envisioned her own co-workers at the paper talking about "taffies" at their weekly staff meeting.

"Are you a police officer, sir?" Joe asked from his seat as their laughter finally died down.

"Call me Mitch. And yeah, I'm a detective."

"I guess you guys like to get away from the real world, huh?"

"Why do you say that?"

"The last guy I brought into town was a cop, too." Joe pulled in the reins as they approached a small hill. "He didn't seem to want to talk much, so I let him be. I imagine you guys have pretty stressful jobs. Especially nowadays."

Elise fell silent as Mitch and the driver continued to talk. There was something hypnotic about the sound of the sleigh bells and the gait of the horses. It was almost as if the quiet, snow-covered path led to a place where all sense of time and worry was wiped away. In fact, if she didn't know any better, she would think she was on a totally deserted island. They hadn't passed a single soul or seen a house since they left the airport.

A low, soft whistle broke through her thoughts and she looked up at Mitch.

"Whoa. Would you look at that place? Wouldn't that be an awesome vacation home? Tucked away behind those big trees you almost wouldn't know it was there. Now *that's* leaving the world behind."

She looked in the direction Mitch was pointing, the corner of the familiar log cabin just visible through the lowest branches of a tall evergreen. The years that had come and gone since she'd last seen it evaporated into thin air. It hadn't changed one bit. She swiped quickly at the tears that threatened to spill down her cheeks, fearful that Mitch would see them, desperate to keep that aspect of her life a secret.

She was a fool for thinking she could come here and forget.

TWO

4:00 p.m.

ELISE PEERED AT her reflection in the antique oval mirror above the mahogany dresser. The sleigh ride to the inn had brought a healthy glow to her cheeks and her blue eyes sparkled despite the unexpected trip down memory lane.

She breathed in deeply, willed herself to focus on today. She was in the middle of a winter wonderland with a man she'd fallen in love with. Lord knew she had done her best to change the past—but it hadn't been enough. It was time to move on. Unfortunately, her heart wasn't always in sync with her head.

Her hand instinctively reached for the tiny heart-shaped locket that hung from the delicate gold chain around her neck. Mitch's Christmas gift was so much more than a pretty necklace. It was a pledge of sorts. A promise.

"You have my heart, Elise."

Those words, that moment, would be etched in her mind for the rest of her life.

Muted voices from the hallway forced her attention back to the present. She studied herself in the mirror, pleased at the way the turquoise-colored sweater set off her eyes and complemented the gold locket. A quick scrunching motion of her hands proved to be just what was needed to revive her curly brown locks.

With a final glance at her image, Elise turned and walked to the door that connected her room with Mitch's. She raised her fist and knocked softly.

"C'mon in, Elise."

She gently turned the doorknob and pushed. The butterflies that took flight in her stomach whenever she knew she was going to see Mitch scrambled into action.

He was there, waiting, sitting on the edge of his bed. He grinned and patted the spot next to him. "How's your room?"

"It's perfect. This whole place is perfect." She sat down beside him. "Do *you* like it?"

She felt his arm slip around her waist, smiled as he gave her a gentle squeeze.

"What's not to like?"

She looked up at his face, felt her body tingle as he flashed his gorgeous smile at her. "And you're really okay with the separate room thing?"

"Am I thrilled? No. But I understand. It's important to you, so it's important to me." He kissed her temple lightly. "But I'd be lying if I said it was easy."

"Thank you." She squeezed his hand. "So, what've you been doing while I was in my room just now?"

"I was looking at this." He picked up a leaflet from the nightstand and ran his finger down the page, stopping midway. "It lists the different services on the island."

"Anything interesting?"

"Actually, yeah. Small world stuff. I know one of the island's two police officers. Brad Matthews and I went to college together."

"Were you friends?"

"Yeah, we hung out quite a bit. He played on the baseball team with me for a year or so."

"You lost touch?"

"You know how guys are. Anyways, I was wondering if you'd mind stopping by the police station after dinner tonight."

Elise tilted her head up slightly and met Mitch's questioning eyes with a smile. "Sounds great. I'd love to meet one of your college buddies—find out some of your secrets."

"I don't have any secrets. What you see is what you get."

Three
4:55 p.m.

SNOW PELTED HIS face as he stared at the block-lettered sign, waiting for some sort of emotion to take hold.

It was inconceivable to him why anyone would want to live in a place like this. Certainly not someone whose livelihood was based on others.

But he'd vowed from the beginning that he wouldn't try to get in their heads. There was no reason to. They were wrong. All of them.

And it was up to him to see that they paid. Especially this one.

"All in good time." The words were whipped from his lips, lost in the biting wind. This was the part he loved. The planning. The plotting.

He took one last look at the building, at the lamp light streaming from the corner window. A light that would be snuffed out soon. Very soon.

Smiling, he turned and headed toward the restaurant at the end of the snow-covered lane.

Four
5:00 p.m.

THE COUNTLESS POLAROID pictures taped to the walls of the small restaurant filled the room with a sense of warmth, a stark irony to the deepening cold and mounting snow outside. Elise studied the pictures above their table, soaking up the myriad of faces.

"What can I get you folks?"

She turned and saw the fifty-something waitress standing beside their table with a pen poised above a small order pad. Elise looked quickly at Mitch and shrugged her shoulders slightly. "I'm sorry, Mitch. I haven't even looked at the menu yet. I was so busy looking at all these pictures that I kind of forgot where I was."

"No problem, kids. I'll give you a few more moments to make up your mind." The woman put her pad and pen into her apron pocket. "I take pictures of every new face that comes into my restaurant during a particular season. The pictures above your table are the start of this year's winter season."

Elise looked again at the photographs on the wall beside their table. "That's a really neat idea. I bet you get quite a few repeat customers that way. People like to see themselves and it probably makes them feel more connected to this restaurant than one that doesn't do this."

"You got it exactly," the woman said, a smile of appreciation creeping across her face as she met Elise's eye. She pointed to the various groupings around the dining area. "I started this about fifteen years ago—just because I love taking pictures and meeting new people. Back then, I'd leave them in a basket by the register and people would shuffle through them out of curiosity. After a while someone suggested I put them on the wall, and so I gave it a shot. Before long I noticed my business increasing. I attributed it to the picture wall. The rest is history, as you can see."

Mitch motioned toward a picture with a group of men raising beer mugs and making finger gestures over each other's heads. "I bet they were a fun group."

The woman laughed. "They are. Most of them anyway. Those guys arrived a few days ago for a competition they're holding today. Something about maps and points and a $4,000 prize."

"Orienteering?" Mitch asked.

"Yes, that's it. Do you know what that is?"

"Sure. You're given a map, a compass, and a set of coordinates. You race each other to see who can find their points in the quickest time. It's fun. I used to do it with a group of buddies in college once in a while." Mitch turned and looked at the group of men in the photograph, his brows furrowed. "But it's not usually something you do in the snow."

"They're doing it on cross country skis." The woman reached across the table and straightened a cockeyed picture.

"Man, that sounds awesome. Wish I knew how to ski already."

"I suspect, with the storm we've got comin', that you'll have lots of opportunity to practice over the next few days." The woman stopped talking for a moment as she focused on the front door. "Seems I have another brave soul searching for a warm dinner. Why don't you look over those menus and I'll be back in a few moments. My name's Sophie."

Elise glanced at the man waiting to be seated. Every inch of his parka was covered with snow. Ice crystals clung to his thick beard, snow matted the tiny scrap of brown hair that escaped from beneath the tightly drawn hood. And although she couldn't see his face, an inexplicable chill ran down her spine.

"You okay, Elise?"

She pulled her gaze from the stranger and focused on Mitch. "What? Oh, yeah, I'm fine. Just a little chilled all of a sudden."

"What looks good to you?" Mitch gestured toward the menu in his hand.

Elise scanned the choices printed on the tri-fold paper. "I think I'm just gonna have a bowl of soup. Maybe it'll help warm me up a little bit." She pulled her sweater closer to her body and shivered again.

Sophie reappeared beside their table and looked at Elise with motherly eyes. "Are you cold, honey?"

"I'll be fine," Elise answered softly. "I guess I just wasn't expecting the island to be this cold."

"I think it's a shock to many folks, but at least you came in wearing a warm coat. I had a young man in here earlier with just a blanket wrapped around him if you can believe it." The woman shook her head slowly and reached into her apron, pulled a notebook and pen from its pocket. "So what did you two kids decide on?"

Elise ordered chicken soup and a cup of hot chocolate; Mitch ordered a bowl of chili.

"I'll get that right out to you."

Within moments the woman was at their table again, this time with warm cups of chocolate for both of them. "Where you kids staying?"

Mitch took a quick sip of his drink and set it back on the table. "The Island Inn. We just got here a few hours ago."

"Nice hotel, you'll like it. And if the snow keeps at the pace it's falling right now, you'll be spending a lot of time there."

Elise looked at the mounting snow outside the restaurant window. In just the short time she and Mitch had been inside, the roadway was completely covered.

"How much snow are they talking about?" Mitch asked.

"Last I heard they were predicting up to two feet of snow with a second wave expected less than twenty-four hours after the first blast." Sophie looked at the snow and shrugged. "If the storm is even half of what they're saying, you kids will be spending a lot more time with us than you originally planned."

The lights in the restaurant flickered.

"What's the power situation over here when a storm like this hits?"

It was as if Mitch had read her mind. Elise watched Sophie's face as the woman considered the question.

"The last time we had a storm like this was about eight years ago. The entire island lost power and phone lines for a good three or four days."

"But you've got back-up generators, don't you?" Mitch asked.

"Oh no. Nobody does. People out here prefer things to stay as simple and rustic as possible. That's why most of the hotel rooms have fireplaces and everyone has a kerosene heater."

Mitch whistled softly under his breath. "Wow. So a storm like this could be pretty serious."

"Don't worry. I've got a propane stove in the kitchen for just this kind of storm, so I'll be open all day no matter what the weather brings. Well, except between two and four. That's my one break each day."

Eerie. It was just as Madame Mariah had predicted during Elise's palm reading last summer. Here she was with Mitch on an isolated island. A blizzard, like Sophie was describing, would certainly qualify as "an eventful trip."

"I'll leave you two kids alone for a few moments and go check on your food. Drink your cocoa, it'll warm you up."

Elise watched Sophie disappear into the kitchen, her thoughts suddenly back in Madame Mariah's House of Fortunes. Could the psychic really have mystical powers after all?

She shook her head gently, forced her mind into the present. And onto Mitch.

Looking into his eyes, she saw a sparkle of amusement. "What? What's so funny?"

"I know what you're thinking, Elise. But just because Mariah said 'eventful,' doesn't mean we can't have an absolute blast. Right?"

He was right. A few extra days together would be a dream come true.

THE SOUP DID the trick. The chill that had seemed to cling to her from the moment the snow-covered stranger entered the restaurant was finally gone. Unfortunately, dinner was over and it was time to head back into the snowy night air. Elise put her arms into the coat Mitch held out for her and buttoned the front all the way up. They headed for the door, past the stranger who sat hunched over his food, reading the local paper Sophie had placed on his table.

"Wait!"

Elise and Mitch turned. Sophie was walking toward them, a camera in hand.

"Heading back to the hotel already?"

"In a little while. First, we're gonna stop by the police station."

"Is everything okay?" Crease lines appeared across Sophie's forehead as she looked at them.

"Everything's fine. Brad Matthews is an old college buddy and I was kinda hoping to surprise him," Mitch said, pulling on his left glove. "Is the station easy to find?"

Sophie nodded, a warm smile replacing the momentary concern in her eyes. "Sure is. Take a right when you head out the door. Go two blocks. Turn left at the next alleyway. The station will be up just a little ways on your right."

"Thanks, Sophie." Mitch turned to Elise, placed his hand on the small of her back. "Ready to go?"

Before she could answer him, Sophie spoke.

"Oh no, you don't. You kids can't leave until I get your picture."

Mitch's arm slid around Elise's waist and pulled her in for a hug. "How's this?"

"Perfect!" The woman snapped their picture. "Unfortunately, you'll probably be gone by the time I get your picture on the wall. My Polaroid camera broke last night so I'm using a regular camera today."

"That's okay." Elise smiled warmly at the woman. There was something very endearing about Sophie. She was the kind of woman you could sit across a table from and gab with for hours. Like Mitch's Aunt Betty. "With any luck we'll be back again someday. Maybe we can see it then."

"Absolutely. Once a picture is up, it stays up."

Five
7:30 p.m.

"SOPHIE WASN'T KIDDING, was she?" Mitch slid his arm around Elise's back and guided her through a pile of newly fallen snow outside the island's small brick police station. "It looks like we've gotten at least six inches since we left the hotel. And I think that's a pretty conservative guess."

"If it keeps falling like this, we'll be snowed in for a month."

The sound of her sweet laugh made him wish that would be the case. A month without mundane paperwork and petty theft cases would be awesome. And to spend it with Elise...

He stopped outside the stationhouse window and peered inside. Brad Matthews was doing exactly what Brad Matthews had done all through college-- skating by. If only Mitch had brought his camera. A picture of Brad sleeping on duty, feet outstretched on the desk in front of him, would be a great addition to the next alumni magazine. He laughed out loud at the image.

"What's so funny?"

Mitch pointed at Brad. "He's got the life of a prince, even now."

"Maybe he's had a tough day," Elise suggested.

"Deciding what to eat for breakfast constitutes a tough day for Brad."

"Mitch! That's not nice."

He ducked to miss her playful swing and grabbed hold of her hand instead. "Watch this, Elise."

He quietly opened the door and stepped inside the station.

"Nice to see our tax dollars are being put toward such good use, young man," Mitch said loudly, disguising his voice to sound older.

The sound of wood scraping wood echoed through the room as the blond, uniformed man nearly fell out of his chair in an effort to rise to his feet.

"Wh—I was just taking a quick break. What can I do for you this evening?" Brad said.

Mitch watched in amusement as a look of recognition began to creep across his buddy's face. "Gotcha!"

"Jesus, Mitch. You scared the crap out of me." Brad leaned back against his desk and raised his hand to his head.

"Sorry. I couldn't resist." Mitch walked across the room and held out his hand. "How ya doing?"

"Aside from the heart attack you just gave me? I'm fine. What are you doing here?"

"Vacation. I noticed your name on an information sheet at the hotel. I couldn't miss an opportunity to stop by and say hello, could I?"

"Maybe you should have," Brad said. He reached out and grabbed hold of Mitch's head in a playful headlock.

"Okay, okay. I'm sorry. I just couldn't forgive myself if I let your powernap go unchecked." He felt Brad's grip on his head loosen and he pulled away.

"Glad I could help your conscience there, pal." Brad straightened the collar on his uniform shirt. "Seriously though, it's great to see you. When did you get here?"

Mitch watched Brad's eyes move past his face, settle on Elise still standing just inside the doorway. He turned and reached for her hand, pulled her close.

"We got here a few hours ago." He looked back at Brad and smiled. "Brad Matthews, I'd like you to meet my girlfriend, Elise Jenkins."

The look of blatant approval that crossed Brad's face wasn't missed by Mitch. And judging by Elise's red cheeks, it wasn't missed by her either.

"It's nice to meet you, Brad." Elise extended her hand and shook Brad's gently.

"It's real nice to meet you, too. You must be somebody special to have captured this guy's heart."

"She is." Mitch pulled Elise's hand to his mouth and kissed her cold skin. Surprised, he looked around the room, his gaze stopping on the far end of the station room. "Man, Brad, isn't this island cold enough for you without having to leave the window open?"

"You know what they say about people who like to be cold."

"No, what?"

"I'm not sure. But I'm sure they say somethin'."

"That's what I thought." Mitch laughed and shook his head. "Some things never change."

"Consistency is part of my charm. The chicks dig it." Brad pulled two chairs over to his desk, then walked around to sit in his own. "So, what are you doing here? I figured you'd be at the FBI or somethin' by now."

Mitch sat down beside Elise. "Why do you say that?"

"I read about those murders you solved last year in Jersey." Brad leaned back in his chair and popped a Tic Tac in his mouth. "I wasn't surprised, though. You were always an overachiever. And I know how you are about not letting the bad guys get away."

"You're *reading* now? When'd you learn how?" Mitch laughed as a Tic Tac flew past his head.

"Seriously man, that must have been one crazy time, huh?"

Damn it. Mitch had really thought they could put all of that behind them, especially this far from home. But he was obviously wrong.

"Yeah, it was crazy." Mitch looked at Elise quickly, watched her eyes cloud over briefly. "But that's all over now."

25

Brad stopped inhaling Tic Tacs long enough to stare at Elise with wide eyes. "Hey, wait a minute. Were you involved in that whole thing, too?"

"Yeah. I'm a reporter for the Ocean Point Weekly and I guess you could say I kind of got wrapped up in the whole thing." She shifted in her seat.

"Reporter? Were you the one who wrote that article when it was all over?"

Elise nodded.

"Wow! That sure ended up in some big time papers, didn't it?" Brad puffed his cheeks out momentarily and swung his gaze from Elise to Mitch. "So you two decided to get away for a few days, huh?"

Mitch heard Elise exhale deeply before she finally answered. "I got some reward money after the case was solved and decided I could use a little bit of a vacation."

"I can imagine." Brad leaned forward in his chair. "We don't have to worry about stuff like that here."

"I'm banking on that." Elise smiled, her familiar sparkle returning. "The brochures I got in the mail sounded heavenly. And so here we are."

"Well, I'm glad. Even if it means having to put up with doofus here," Brad said, looking at Mitch. "It's funny, we've always been popular in the summertime, yet no one ever seemed to think about us once October rolled around. But that started to change about two years ago when one of the locals came up with marketing the island as a winter paradise. It's still relatively quiet in the winter, but we've started attracting cross country skiers and a decent number of honeymooners."

"The info sheet back at the room said there's just two of you out here." Mitch looked around the room. Both desks, a few filing cabinets, and a tiny waiting area just about filled every square inch of the room.

"Yup. My partner's on vacation, too. Somewhere in the Caribbean, the lucky dog."

"Think you can handle things by yourself?" Mitch asked. The teasing felt so natural, like they hadn't missed a beat since college.

"Don't knock it till you try it, Mitch. I get my fair share of calls from distressed citizens."

"Can't get their horses hitched to the sled?"

"Ha, ha, ha. You've got it all wrong. They call me when they can't get their sled out of a ditch."

The ringing of the telephone brought an abrupt end to the laughter in the room. Brad waved his right hand in the air, then reached for his desk phone.

"Mackinac Island Police Department. This is Officer Brad Matthews, how can I help you?"

It didn't take long for Mitch to realize the call was important. Brad's face showed definite signs of tension as he listened to the caller.

"What makes you think he's on our island?"

Looking quickly in Elise's direction, Mitch could sense that she, too, felt the unspoken urgency that now blanketed the tiny police station.

"Agent Walker, as you know this is a very small, secluded island. Particularly at this time of year. I'm one of only two officers assigned to this station, and my co-worker is out of the country. But a college friend of mine is visiting the island and he's sitting right here. He's a detective from New Jersey. Should we bring him in on this?"

"What's going on, Brad?" Mitch murmured, jumping to his feet. He glanced at the pad of paper Brad was using for notes.

Brad shot his index finger into the air quickly and pulled the phone closer to his ear.

"Detective Burns' girlfriend is in the station as well, but that's it."

Mitch shrugged at Elise's questioning eyes.

"Okay. Let me put you on speaker," Brad said. He pressed the small black button at the bottom of the phone and motioned to Mitch. "Okay, sir. Go ahead."

"Detective Burns, my name is Agent Bud Walker with the FBI. As I was telling Officer Matthews a moment ago, we have good reason to believe a serial killer may be hiding on your island as we speak."

Mitch's stomach muscles tightened, his grip on the corner of the desk intensified. This couldn't be happening.

"We've been tracking this scumbag across three states as he leaves a body behind in each location. He's a tough one to find because he changes his appearance so often, taking the vocation of each new victim."

"Vocation?" Brad asked.

"Yeah. He kills a teacher, he pretends he's a teacher. He kills a counselor, he pretends he's a counselor," the agent explained.

"What makes you think he's here?" Mitch asked. He rubbed his palm down his face as he waited for the agent's reply.

"The last report we have as to his whereabouts puts him within easy reach of Mackinac Island. Which, from all accounts, would be the perfect place to hide right now with the storm you're getting."

"We've already got somethin' like eight inches and it's still coming down fast and furiously," Brad replied.

Mitch turned to look outside. There was no doubt about it. This would be an ideal place for a killer to hide, to regroup.

"What role do you want us to play?" Brad continued.

"You may very well be handling this whole thing for right now. The snow is so bad that we can't fly in at this point. If we get a break in the weather, we'll do our best, but—"

"The runway out here will be a mess," Brad finished aloud.

"That's what they're telling me. Anyway, I need your fax number so I can send you a couple of the drawings we've gotten from witnesses along the way."

"Great." Brad gave him the fax number to the station.

Mitch listened as the FBI agent repeated the number, his mind whirling around the task in front of them.

"Agent Walker, are there any particular traits or mannerisms this guy has that might help us pick him out? Do you think he'll try to hide from the authorities?" Mitch asked.

"This guy is as brazen as they come. He'll be right under your nose. That's half the thrill for this loser. Hold on, let me put this into the fax."

Within seconds the station's dedicated fax line rang and the sound of paper feeding through the machine echoed against the cinderblock walls.

"I'll get it." Elise rushed to the small desk in the back corner of the room.

"Is it coming through?" the agent asked.

"As we speak," Mitch answered.

"We gotta get this scumbag, boys. His last victim was a—"

Silence filled the stationhouse, as the caller's voice and accompanying background sounds ceased simultaneously.

"Was a what?" Mitch asked quickly. "Agent Walker, are you still there?"

Brad rapidly pressed the button on the telephone, his shoulders rigid with tension. "Damn it! The phone's dead!"

The feeling of helplessness that enveloped the room was magnified as the station's lights flickered briefly then went out, leaving the threesome in total darkness.

"Crap." The sound of a drawer opening and things being pushed around filled the otherwise silent room. "Hang on, guys, I've got a flashlight here somewh— Damn!"

"You okay, Brad?" Mitch asked.

"Uh, yeah. Scraped my hand on something in the drawer. Wait, here it is."

A beam of light suddenly shone across the room, stopped on Elise and the fax machine.

"The fax stopped, too," Elise said, her voice panicked.

In a second Mitch was by her side, yanking the paper out of the machine.

"Did we get anything to go on before the lines went dead?" Brad asked.

"He's got hair." Mitch dropped the piece of paper onto the floor and slammed his fist down on the table. "We've got reason to believe there's a psychopath on this island and we don't know anything about him. Except that he's not bald—at least not at the time this particular sketch was drawn. The only thing we *do* know is that we might be stranded on an island with this killer during the snowstorm from hell."

"Agent Walker said that he takes the vocation of his victims." Brad's words were of little help and they all knew it.

"But the line went dead before the agent could tell us who the last victim was." Elise picked the incomplete fax off the ground and tossed it onto a nearby desk. "And Mitch is right. This drawing—or lack of one—isn't going to help shed any light on who we're looking for."

"What now?" Brad asked, his voice a clear giveaway of the fear gripping them all. "This kind of thing just doesn't happen here. I was only semi-joking when I said my police calls are pretty much confined to helping a neighbor out of a ditch."

Mitch rubbed his palm down his face and took a deep breath. The calmness that was his during a crisis was returning. Finally.

"What we need to do is take a deep breath and come up with some sort of plan to keep everyone safe until this thing is over." Mitch looked straight into Brad's eyes, willed his college buddy to get it together somehow. "There is still a chance this guy never made it onto the island."

"And if he did?" Brad asked.

"If he did, it's possible he'll simply choose to hide."

"Hide?"

"Yeah. So he can slip out a little easier when the storm ends."

"I hope you're right, Mitch."

So do I, he thought.

"Excuse me."

Mitch turned, his gaze riveted on the man standing in the doorway shielding his eyes from Brad's flashlight.

"I'm sorry. We didn't hear you come in." Brad squared his shoulders and lowered the flashlight's beam. "How can I help you?"

"My name's Dan Friar. I need to report a missing person."

He was careful to stay in the shadows near the window, yet he was still close enough to hear everything that was said inside. The frustration in Agent Walker's voice was invigorating, the power failure a dream come true. The storm was proving to be everything he'd hoped and more.

Sure, he hadn't counted on the detective from New Jersey being in the mix, but it didn't matter now. They didn't have a clue who he was or what he looked like.

And a missing person on top of everything? How perfect was that?

He bit down hard on his lower lip to stifle the laugh that threatened to blow his cover. He couldn't have orchestrated things any better. Satisfied, he tightened the drawstring on his hood and began walking toward the small inn at the end of the alleyway.

Six
10:00 p.m.

SHE HATED SEEING Mitch under so much stress. Hated the fact that the vacation they so desperately needed was turning into something out of a horror movie. But it was what it was. Hating it wasn't going to change it. Elise knew she needed to support Mitch and Brad in every way possible. But it was hard.

The power had been out for nearly an hour now. Mitch and Brad were talking to Dan Friar near the kerosene heater. The absolute certainty she felt about the serial killer's hand in the skier's disappearance was mirrored in Mitch's face. He was painstakingly taking Dan Friar through every moment of the orienteering competition leading up to the time when the victim was first discovered missing.

"What we need to do is gather as many volunteers as possible for a search party at daybreak." Mitch's words filtered through her thoughts, forced her to focus on the crisis once again. "Let's meet at eight tomorrow morning, right outside the station."

"I think we should have everyone meet outside Sophie's Place instead," Brad suggested. "Being on a side path like this, most visitors have no idea where the police station is. But just about everyone can find their way to Sophie's."

Mitch nodded.

It was obvious to Elise that his mind was already on the next step. "Can I do something, Mitch?"

"Brad, why don't you give that pad of paper to Elise. We need to come up with a list of people to help with the search."

Elise took the pad and a pencil from Brad's outstretched hand and scooted her chair closer to the flashlight.

"How'll we get word to everyone if we don't have working phones?" Dan Friar asked.

"Not a problem," Brad said. "Sophie lives in an apartment above her restaurant. She serves breakfast starting at seven, no matter what the weather. She'll cook by a propane grill if she has to."

"It still blows me away that you guys don't have generators out here," Mitch said, tapping a pen on the top of Brad's desk.

"We haven't been doing the winter tourism thing for very long. And most of our locals want things to stay simple, rustic. And as stupid as it sounds, that means no generators."

"Do you really think many people will come out to a restaurant in these kinds of conditions?" Elise asked quietly.

"My bet is that most visitors will be holed up in their hotel rooms, doing their best to avoid the snow. All of our hotels are required—in winter—to have a supply of non-perishable food and drinks on hand in the event of a storm like this," Brad said. "But the locals, they'll brave just about any storm you throw at them. And there's two things you can count on around here regardless of the weather—Sophie's, coffee on a Friday morning, and the fact that she takes her break every day between two and four."

"Most of my orienteering club is staying at the same hotel I am. When I tell them about the search, they'll want to help find Pete," Dan Friar interjected. "And they already know where the restaurant is."

Elise looked down at her still-empty pad of paper and considered Dan's words. If the group was so worried about Pete then why—

"Dan?"

"Yeah?"

"What time did the competition start this morning?" Elise asked, her mind suddenly reeling with questions.

"Officially? About 11:30."

She felt Mitch's eyes on her as she continued asking questions.

"Then why did you wait 'til now to report him as missing?"

"We figured he was just pissed at himself for losing and went back to his room."

"Was he the type to sulk when he lost?" Elise asked.

Dan leaned back in his chair, fiddled with a paperweight on Brad's desk. When he spoke, his voice was quiet and unsure.

"Don't know. He never lost."

"Never?"

Dan shook his head slowly, exhaled loudly.

"Never. He was a fierce competitor. And since these events are about friendly competition, he'd motivate himself by continually trying to beat his own time."

"Did the other guys resent him for always winning?" Elise asked, jotting notes on her pad.

"You'd think they would, wouldn't you? But no one did. Everyone liked Pete. He was a nice guy." Dan turned his head and looked out the window into the darkness, his eyes tired and vacant. "Do you know what he was gonna do with the prize money?"

Realizing Dan was talking as much to himself as to them, Elise stopped writing and waited for the man to continue.

"He was gonna take his wife on a second honeymoon. He'd been planning it for months. But he didn't tell anyone except me. He didn't want to run the chance someone would let him win. He wanted to win her that trip all on his own."

Elise rolled the pencil between her fingers, replayed Dan's words in her mind as a new question popped into her head.

"Why did he tell you?"

"Because we're friends. We hit it off the first time we met. I understood his need to leave work behind, and he understood my desire to grow this group even when the rest of the guys wanted things to stay the same."

Listening from the sidelines for much of the conversation, Mitch finally spoke. "So what made you decide he was missing?"

"When he didn't answer his phone or open the door for dinner. We stood outside his door and taunted him, tried pushing all the buttons we could think of to make him come out of his room. When he didn't respond, I started to worry. He had heart problems, you know. We pleaded with the hotel manager to open the door and let us check on him. When she did, Pete wasn't there."

"What kind of equipment did Pete have with him for the competition?" Mitch asked.

"The standard stuff. Heavy waterproof parka, skis, a map of the course." Dan closed his eyes as he continued to run through Pete's inventory of gear. "He also had a thermos and that new high-speed compass he just got. The thing was a beaut."

"Were any of those items in the hotel room when the manager let you in?" Elise asked softly.

Dan shook his head. "No. Not that we saw, anyway. His breakfast trash was still on the nightstand. And Pete is beyond neat. He's a perfectionist."

Elise jotted a few more notes then looked back at Dan. She saw the worry in the man's tired eyes. Without thinking, she reached across the desk and patted his clenched hand.

"Pray."

Dan nodded, his voice quiet. "I haven't stopped since we realized he was missing."

Mitch cleared his throat and stood. "Can we count on you, Dan, to round up the orienteering guys for the search?"

"Absolutely."

"Perfect." Mitch looked at Elise momentarily and gestured toward the pad of paper in front of her. "In addition to looking for Pete, we've also got to start thinking of ways to protect everyone."

He walked toward the open window and stood, looking out into the night for a moment before turning around. "Brad, let's say our guy is here. Is there anyone, for whatever reason, who may be particularly vulnerable to a sicko like this?"

She waited, her hand poised to write any names Brad would mention.

"The only one that really jumps to mind is a guy who lives in a cabin out by the airport. He's a recluse. You know, a hermit. I've been here for about five years now and I haven't laid eyes on him even once. His name's Fogarty. Old man Fogarty."

Elise heard the snap of her pencil, felt the splintered wood dig into her palm as Brad's words washed over her like ice water.

Friday, January 28th
Seven
8:00 a.m.

MITCH LOOKED INTO the faces of the group assembled in front of him. Brad was right. Sophie's Place had been the perfect way to get the word out on the search. The only dilemma now was how to find someone in the woods with nearly thirteen inches of snow on the ground and more falling every moment.

"My name is Mitch Burns, and I'd like to thank all of you for coming out this morning. Officer Matthews and I need all the help we can get with the elements we're facing." Mitch cleared his throat. "Pete Garner has been out in this blizzard since yesterday morning. Time is not on his side."

The looks that passed between the men in front of him were a mixture of apprehension and curiosity. But Mitch knew that the best way to thwart panic was to share as many details as he could. Knowledge is power as Aunt Betty always said.

"I've got a photograph here of the orienteering group. Pete's the third one in on the left. It'll give you an idea of who we're looking for, but I don't think we're gonna find many people wandering aimlessly in this weather."

Mitch turned and looked at Dan Friar. "Is there anything you want to share with these folks before we head out?"

Dan Friar moved alongside Mitch and Brad. "Pete Garner is about my height. He's got that salt and pepper color hair and it's receding along his part line. He's about twenty pounds lighter than I am and is a fierce competitor. He was wearing a dark brown parka with black leather gloves the last time we saw him. He should have his compass with him, but in this snow he may have become disoriented."

Mitch searched the face of each and every man standing in front of them as Dan continued his description of Pete Garner. It wasn't hard to pick out the orienteering club members. They were all huddled together, a unified look of determination etched in their faces. Only this time it wasn't about finding the most points in the quickest time. It was about finding their friend.

Mitch's gaze fell on a well-built man standing just to the right of the orienteering members. He seemed to be alone— separate from the group of locals, not part of the orienteering club.

Dan stopped talking and all eyes turned back to Mitch. He willed his gaze to move off the loner and back onto the group as a whole.

"Sophie's been generous enough to fill a thermos with hot coffee for each of us." Mitch straightened his arm directly in front of him. "Everyone left of my arm will be searching with Officer Matthews. Everyone to the right will be searching with Dan Friar and myself. Each team has a set of whistles that are to be blown only in the event of an emergency, or if you find Pete Garner."

Sophie and Elise stepped out of the restaurant with an armful of thermoses for the searchers and began handing them out.

Mitch took the opportunity to pull Dan aside and inquire about the red-haired loner. "Do you have any idea who that guy is?"

"His name's Mark. Don't know him very well, except that he's a firefighter from some place out west. He showed up yesterday for the competition and ended up winning the damn thing."

"First impression?"

"I'd say quiet, maybe a little standoffish."

Mitch nodded, watched the man take a thermos and move into his designated group. The one Mitch was leading.

Dan's voice continued in his ear.

"But he does have one helluva temper, that's for sure."

Mitch's gaze moved off Mark and back onto Dan. "Why do you say that?"

"See that guy over there?" Dan raised his hand and pointed to a short, stocky guy who appeared to be in his early to mid-twenties.

Mitch nodded.

"His name's Josh. Got real pissy when Mark won yesterday. Started cursing and kicking at the snow. It was really kind of funny."

Mitch snorted. There were just some things you could tell about a person at first glance. And Dan's description of Josh's childish behavior came as little surprise.

"What was his problem?"

"I don't know, but he was hollerin' about his ex-wife and how she was draining him or some crap like that. You know, violin playin' stuff."

Mitch knew the type all right. Sounded like a few of the rookies in his department during the morning run.

"Anyway, Mark got real angry when Josh started acting like that. Called him a sore loser, asked him if he wanted to make an issue of it." Dan shook his head and lowered his voice. "We all told him to let it go, that Joshie Boy is just like that. But he just couldn't seem to shake it off. And since none of us knew him, we didn't worry about it too much. Figured he'd let it go, or else we'd all have a ring-side seat for a doozy of a fight."

Mitch looked at Mark once again, studied the rigid way the newcomer held his shoulders. He was glad Mark was on his search team. It would be the perfect opportunity to keep an eye on him.

"Are you ready to head out, Mitch?"

A hand on his arm pulled his attention away from Mark.

He reached for the thermos Elise held out for him and looked into her sunken blue eyes. She'd been so quiet, so withdrawn since they'd left the station last night. He'd heard her pacing in her room for hours after she shut the door. This whole situation had to be a painful reminder of the terror she'd endured last summer. A terror he'd promised himself she would never know again.

Mitch pulled her in for a hug. "I'll be okay, Elise. Just stay here with Sophie and keep your eyes open." He pushed a strand of hair off her forehead and kissed her quickly. "I gotta go."

He fell in step with the members of his search party, a few paces behind Mark. Knowing his gun was in a holster beneath his coat helped. Especially now.

HIS INSULATED GLOVES were little match for the biting cold. Two hours of searching had yielded nothing. The snow was mounting, making their efforts futile at best.

Mitch looked around at the men assigned to his search party. Their failure to find any explanation as to Pete's whereabouts weighed heavily on their faces. They needed a break of some kind. A footprint, a shred of clothes, the guy's compass, something. But even if it were here, they wouldn't find it. Not in all this snow.

Mitch stopped beside an enormous fir tree and opened his thermos. He swallowed the last gulp of coffee, the now lukewarm liquid doing little to dispel the chill in his body. He had to wrap it up. The last thing they needed was to lose anyone else. He wiped his mouth on his sleeve and looked over at Dan, who was standing just a few feet away

"Dan, I'm afraid we're gonna have to call it quits for now. Everyone needs to rest, warm up, get into some dry clothes." He could sense the disappointment behind the man's slow nod.

Mitch looked down at his feet at the thermos cap he'd just dropped. His hands were becoming numb inside the gloves, a sure sign that frostbite was just around the corner. He had to end the search.

Sighing, Mitch bent down to pick up the green plastic cap. As his gloved hand brushed the wet snow, his gaze fell on a tiny scrap of brown material. He fell to his knees and began digging at the smaller pile of snow near the base of the tree.

Dan dropped down beside him and began digging, too.

The biting cold that had made Mitch's fingers so numb just moments earlier, suddenly seemed powerless against the determination coursing through his body.

Within moments, the dark brown fabric removed any hope that Pete's disappearance was an accident.

The body of Pete Garner, a hideous shade of blue, sprawled out in front of them. The same parka that had once protected him from the elements had done little to shield him from the wrath of a killer.

Mitch silently counted each blood-encrusted slash mark, choked back the bile that rose in his throat as he reached fifteen. Fifteen too many.

He raised the whistle to his lips and blew.

Eight
Noon

IF ONLY SHE could reach across the table and erase the fear from Mitch's eyes, the same fear etched in the faces of the men slumped in chairs around them.

Any hope the serial killer hadn't reached the island was ripped apart the moment Pete's body was discovered. The vicious stab wounds the men reported served as proof of a fact that could no longer be ignored or wished away. And with no power or working phones, they were all sitting ducks at the mercy of a maniac.

Elise's heart ached as she looked around at the small groupings of men throughout Sophie's restaurant. They looked so cold and tired, the defeat on their faces unmistakable. Dan Friar's tablemates were especially quiet. They'd known Pete the longest, felt his loss the deepest. Dan sat staring, his focus on nothing but whatever images he held in his head. Drew rested his head on his forearm; Austin stared into his coffee mug. Josh looked at the faces around him, then at the floor—a sequence he repeated often, interrupted only by an occasional shift in his seat or a clearing of his throat.

She glanced back at Mitch. His uneaten sandwich sat on his plate. His eyes were cloudy, his thoughts a million miles away.

She understood his fear, his grief. But she also knew he needed to regroup.

"We'll get through this, Mitch. By finding Pete so quickly, you've given yourself more time to focus and plan."

He nodded but didn't speak.

"I'll help in any way I can. And Brad will be fine as long as he can follow your lead," she continued.

Mitch leaned across the table and spoke quietly. "That's just it, Lise. Brad needs someone to take the lead and I'm not sure I can do it."

"Of course, you can. You're just tired, in shock. But with some food and a chance to sit, you'll get it together. You have to, Mitch." She hoped her words weren't too strong. She knew the weight that was on his shoulders and didn't want to add to it, but she needed his strength right now. And so did everyone else on the island.

Mitch was silent, his shoulders slumped. Elise looked away, her eyes resting on the photographs beside their table. She took a deep breath and pointed at the picture of the skiers with their beer mugs—the same picture that had caught their eye just yesterday evening. "It's not right that they were so happy two days ago and now are so miserable."

Mitch raised his head and looked at the picture.

"They came here to have some fun and blow off some steam. And now they're under more stress than any desk job could ever cause," she continued.

"Remember what Dan said about Pete? How he was planning to use the prize money to take his wife on a second honeymoon?" Mitch's voice was a near-whisper. "And now we can't even get word to her that her husband is dead."

Elise held her breath. The fight was coming back into Mitch's eyes. She knew its source, knew he was thinking of his dad's murder and the way the killer had eluded police for so long.

She knew the memories were painful for him, but she also knew they had the habit of motivating him in any number of situations. And judging by the way he suddenly straightened in his chair and looked at the pictures on the wall, Elise could see that this was no exception.

"Funny, but I don't see the redhead anywhere."

"Who?" Elise asked.

Mitch pointed at a man sitting by himself in a far corner of the restaurant. "That guy."

"And?"

"And he showed up at the competition yesterday morning and ended up winning the money when Pete disappeared. Everyone was shocked because Pete was the hands-down favorite."

Elise dropped her voice to a near whisper. "Do you think he could be the killer?"

"I don't know. But I've got my eyes on him. He seems real removed from everyone. Real sullen."

"How long has he been on the island?" She studied the man from head to toe, waited for her radar to go off, but it didn't. He simply looked like a guy who wasn't comfortable in his own skin.

"A week or so. Or so he says."

"If he's eaten here then his picture should be on the wall, right?" she asked.

"That's what I'm thinking." Mitch shot his hand in the air and beckoned to the woman making the rounds of each table, coffeepot in hand.

"Need some coffee, Mitch?" Sophie asked. The woman placed a gentle hand on Mitch's shoulder, flashed a look of concern at Elise.

"Actually, Sophie, I could use your memory." Mitch looked at the woman as he spoke, his eyes never leaving her face. "There's a redheaded guy sitting in the corner by the door. Name's Mark. He says he's been here for a while, but I don't see his picture on the wall. Have you ever seen him before?"

Elise saw Sophie turn and look in the direction of the door. Confusion crossed the woman's face as she slowly offered an unreturned wave to a customer who'd just entered the restaurant and stood inches from Mark.

Although Elise couldn't see his face inside the tightly drawn hood, the man's wooden stance seemed vaguely familiar. Shivering suddenly, she forced her attention back to Sophie. The woman stood next to Elise's seat, her eyes closed.

"Sophie?"

The woman opened her eyes slowly but said nothing.

"Sophie?" Mitch asked, his voice gentle yet firm. "You okay?"

"Oh, sorry. I guess I got distracted for a moment. The redhead, right? Yes, he's been in here. Quiet guy. Doesn't have much to say."

"When did you take his picture?" Elise asked.

"I always take a picture of someone on their first visit. I know I took his picture, but I'm not sure why it isn't on the wall."

"Your Polaroid camera was broken when we came in yesterday and you took our picture with a regular camera." Mitch looked up at Sophie as he continued. "I imagine that roll is still sitting in your camera, right?"

Elise shook her head in amazement, watching Mitch's detective skills take over. He was back. They were going to be all right.

"I actually finished that roll right after you left, but can't get it developed because the camera shop is without power just like everyone else." Sophie's voice trailed off as she appeared to mull something over in her head. "Besides, I'm pretty sure *he* was a Polaroid shot."

"But if you took his picture with the Polaroid, it should be here on the wall, right?" Mitch asked.

"I guess..."

It was obvious that the stress of the day was taking a toll on Sophie. The woman's forehead was creased with worry, her eyes dull and sad. Elise knew how she felt. Things like this weren't supposed to happen here.

Elise met Mitch's eye across the table and gave a slight shake before looking back at Sophie.

"Don't worry about it, Sophie. We'll figure it out later." She reached for the woman's hand and gave it a gentle squeeze.

"I'm sorry, kids. I don't mean to be so absent-minded. It's just that..."

"It's okay, Sophie, really." Mitch's voice softened. "Today's been awful for all of us. The picture's not a big deal."

"Thanks, Detective. I guess I should get back to work and make sure these poor men have enough coffee. I imagine they're chilled to the bone right now." Sophie looked around the restaurant, her eyes troubled, her voice quiet. "I'm just not sure what my coffee can do to change the chill in their hearts."

"DETECTIVE BURNS?"

Mitch looked up from the notepad Sophie had loaned him, his mind still focused on the ever-growing list of tasks he and Brad needed to work on that afternoon. "Yes?"

"I'm Jonathan Moore. Retired officer from Cook County Sheriff's Department in southwestern Georgia." The man pulled a badge from his back pocket and held it up for Mitch to see. "I just heard what's going on and wanted to offer some help."

The man's words sliced through Mitch's preoccupation like a knife. He jumped from his seat and extended his hand in one rapid-fire motion, his eyes suddenly riveted on the tall, gray-haired man. "Man, do we ever need some help. I'm Mitch Burns." He motioned to Elise's empty chair. "Sit, sit."

Mitch soaked up every detail of the man, the way he draped his trench coat over the seat back, the way he inhaled sharply through his nose, the way he sat in the chair with an air of authority before speaking.

"I was sick of sitting in my hotel room watching the snow fly past my window so I decided to venture out for a little while. I thought for sure I was the only nut who'd go out in this stuff. Then I looked in the windows here. I couldn't believe all these people."

Mitch sat back down, ran his palm across his face. "Everyone's just trying to get warmed up after being out in that damn snow all morning." His words trailed off as he recalled Pete's blue skin and staring eyes. It was a vision he knew would haunt him for life.

"I asked the big guy sitting over by the door what was going on. He told me about the search and the body. Is it true the guy was murdered?"

Mitch cleared his throat, leaned forward in his chair and swung his gaze in Mark's direction. The skier was still sitting at the same corner table by the door, nursing the same mug of coffee. Alone.

"Detective?"

Most guys like shooting the breeze with other guys. Comparing jobs, talking about women, swapping stupid jokes. So why did the redhead keep to himself? Was he simply a loner? Or was there more?

"Detective Burns?"

Mitch pulled his gaze away from Mark and looked, once again, at the gray-haired man across from him. He saw a mixture of curiosity and frustration in the man's eyes.

"I'm sorry, Jonathan. I guess my mind's on overload right now."

"So it's true?"

He nodded slowly. "Yeah, it's true. And it's pissing me off. I'm so sick of dirt bags like this deciding who should live and who shouldn't. But I'll tell you this—I'm gonna find the guy who did this and make sure he pays."

Jonathan let out a low whistle under his breath and leaned forward, shaking his head. "Any hunches yet?"

Mitch lowered his voice and nodded. "The redhead that sent you over here is really the only one who's raised my suspicion at this point, but it's early. What I *do* know is that he met up with the victim's ski group yesterday morning, won their competition and the four Grand that went along with it. He keeps to himself. No one seems to know anything about him. I'm just not sure if that aloofness is the way he is, or a cover."

"A cover?"

Mitch leaned across the table and dropped his voice to a whisper. "We have reason to believe this murder is more than an   isolated   occurrence."

"Oh?"

"Yeah. The FBI thinks we've got a serial killer on the island."

47

He watched as Jonathan's gaze moved slowly around the room, stopped momentarily to study the lone occupant of the corner table by the door, then came back to rest on Mitch once again. The man's technique was very much like his own—quiet, quick, thorough.

"What do you want me to do?"

"If you're really willing to help, I think we should head over to the police department. You'll need to meet Officer Matthews and then we'll go over a little strategy to get everyone through this. Alive."

"I'm in. You heading over now?"

Mitch pushed back his chair and stood. "Yeah. I gotta grab my girlfriend first. She's in the back with Sophie filling some more thermoses for the guys who helped with the search."

Jonathan shook Mitch's outstretched hand. "Just let me get something warm to drink myself and I'll meet you at the station in a few minutes."

"Thanks, Jonathan."

Nine
2:30 p.m.

MITCH STOOD TO the right of Brad's desk, his gaze traveling the map on the wall. Brad had put a pushpin everywhere a building was located along the main road. Hotels, businesses, library, fire department, newspaper office. But it wasn't those buildings that made him worry so much. It was the scattered pins further inland that were the most appealing spots for someone trying to hide.

"If you notice, I tried to color-coordinate the pins a little bit so you can see what's what." Brad swept his hand across the map, stopped on the row of pushpins that denoted the area around Sophie's. "The tourists are all going to be here, where the blue pins are. I'm thinking we might be able to get a few walkie talkies out to some of those hotels so we can keep in touch with them easier."

Mitch nodded, his mind absorbing everything Brad said.

"But, as you can see, the red and yellow pins are gonna be tougher to monitor, tougher to check." Brad picked up a piece of yellow paper with various notes scrawled across the page. "The red pins are homes. The yellow ones are a few of the outlying businesses."

"What kind of businesses?" Elise asked, her voice quiet but steady.

"Well, this one right here is a livery. It's where the horse-drawn taxis and trail rides are run from. Vic Stodder owns it but has gotten too old to run it on his own. He'd been hoping to get someone who knew about horses to help him out, but that hasn't happened yet to my knowledge. Joe's been carrying most the load, but he also works at the Victorian House Hotel and his mom doesn't want him to quit that job to tend horses all day. And I imagine, with this storm, Joe's working that hotel job twenty-four seven which is leaving Vic high and dry."

"And that one?" Elise pointed to a yellow pushpin off the main outer road.

"That's the rental place. People can rent bikes there during the summer months, cross country skis and snow mobiles in the winter."

Cross country skis.

"That's it!"

Elise and Brad turned from the map at the same moment, their eyes large and questioning.

"Cross country skis! Dan Friar said the killer almost had to have been on skis—and been fairly good at maneuvering on them—in order to get to Pete, kill him, and get out before being noticed."

Brad stood motionless, his eyes glazed in thought.

"Think, Brad. There were skiers all over those woods that morning. Someone not on skis would have stood out." Mitch waited for Brad to catch up, to say something, anything.

"Yeah..."

Exasperated, Mitch pulled his hand across his face and over his hair. "Yeah" wasn't exactly what he was looking for.

Elise's quiet voice filled the room, her words confirmation of the path his mind had begun to take. "If this guy was running from the FBI, he probably wasn't bogged down with much stuff. Most likely he would've picked up skis after he got here."

That's my girl.

Mitch nodded quickly at Elise, then turned his attention to Brad. Sure enough, their train of thought finally pulled into Brad's station.

"Hey! The only place to get skis on the island is the rental shop."

"Bingo!" Mitch felt his shoulders sag in relief. Brad was a good guy, but definitely not the sharpest tack in the box.

"Let's put that on the short list of places to check out." Brad reached for a pad of paper and began to write. "Doug and Michelle live right above the shop so they'll be easy to find."

"We also need to consider the possibility he stole some skis. So keep your ears open for any mention of that," Mitch said.

The jingle of the front door made them turn.

"Hey, Jonathan, glad you found us." Mitch covered the distance between the map and the door in several quick strides. He reached for Jonathan's cold hand and shook it firmly. "Throw your coat on the chair there and let me introduce you to Brad."

Jonathan unzipped his coat and rubbed his hands together. "It's cold out there."

"I'm afraid it's not a whole lot different in here thanks to a window my buddy refuses to shut no matter what the temperature." Mitch turned, cupped his hand on Brad's shoulder. "Jonathan, this is Officer Brad Matthews."

"Are we ever glad you found us." Brad shook Jonathan's hand, a smile temporarily replacing the worried scowl that had been a fixture on his face since Agent Walker's call. "How long have you been here?"

"I got here about a week ago. I've been staying over at Lakeside Inn." Mitch watched as Jonathan's gaze moved to the map on the wall, studied the location of every pushpin. "Who did this?"

"Brad did. He's done a great job of putting this together so that I, and now we, can get a quick feel for the layout of the island." Mitch stepped closer to the map and pointed to the yellow pushpin denoting the equipment rental shop. "I was just saying it might be a good idea to check with the rental shop to see who may have rented cross country skis yesterday morning."

Jonathan's eyes never left the map. "Do you have any way to keep in touch with these people with the phone lines being down?"

"I'm afraid not. Not the outlying buildings anyway. I have a few walkie talkies I thought we might try in some of the bigger hotels. I'm just not sure if the range is gonna be too far." Brad stepped back and leaned against his desk.

Mitch studied the map, his gaze riveted on the spot Brad had circled in black marker. The woods where Pete's body was found. "Besides the ski group, are there any other large groups visiting the island right now?"

"Yeah, I think so." Brad reached across his desk and grabbed a copy of the Island Weekly. He unfolded the paper, turned a few pages, then stopped. "Yup, there's a class reunion group from some college in Louisiana. Most of those folks are staying at the Island Inn where you and Elise are, and the Lakeside Inn where Jonathan is. Why?"

Before Mitch could answer, Jonathan spoke, his words slow but firm. "Because a larger group would be a great place for a guy like ours to assimilate into—at least to an outsider looking in."

Mitch nodded, pleased at Jonathan's quick assessment.

"Man, you guys are gonna be holding my hand through this whole thing. I feel like an idiot." Brad puffed out his cheeks and exhaled loudly.

"You'll be fine, son." Jonathan placed a hand on Brad's shoulder. "No one expects to come up against a situation like this. Certainly not here."

Elise cleared her throat quietly and pointed at the red pushpins that sporadically dotted the island's interior. "What are we gonna do about the people who live in those homes? Is there a way we can make sure they're safe?"

Mitch looked at the map once again, noticed the way Elise's hand lingered on a pin near the airport.

"I'm sorry, I haven't met you." Jonathan reached for Elise's hand. "I'm Jonathan Moore."

"Ah geez, excuse me. I'm sorry. I forgot Elise was in back with Sophie when we met. Jonathan, this is my girlfriend, Elise Jenkins."

Elise's hand disappeared inside Jonathan's firm grasp, her tired eyes held only a hint of their normal sparkle as she smiled up at the man.

"It's very nice to meet you, Jonathan. Thanks so much for helping."

Mitch reached out for Elise and pulled her in for a quick hug. He hated the tension in her body, the fear in her eyes. If only there was somewhere safe she could go to wait this out while he held down the fort with Brad and Jonathan. But there wasn't. And he knew she'd never go. She had way too much spunk to be shipped away.

"Now, what were you saying about the outlying homes?" Jonathan looked at Elise, then gestured to the map.

"I was just thinking out loud more than anything else, I guess. I just can't help but worry about those people being out so far. Alone."

"That's a good point." Mitch looked at his college buddy, still leaning against the desk. "Brad, are there many empty rooms in the hotels right now?"

"I'm sure there are. Winter's not a real busy time for us. If I had to venture a guess, I'd say only half our rooms are full. And that's probably an inflated guess."

"What do you think of rounding up the skiers tomorrow morning and having them go from house to house out there, encouraging those homeowners to stay at one of the hotels where we can keep a better eye on everyone?" Mitch moved his finger from one red pin to another, counting in his head. "I would imagine the homeowners all have skis or a snowmobile to make it through the snow, right?"

Brad appeared to consider Mitch's plan. "Definitely. Everyone's got some way to get around. Of course there are a few who are holed up waiting out the storm and don't have a clue what's going on here."

"Do you think most folks would come?" Jonathan asked.

"If they know what's going on, yeah." Brad pushed off the desk, walked toward the map and pointed at the red pin closest to the runway. "Except him. I suspect he won't even answer the door."

"Why not?" Jonathan asked gruffly.

"He's a hermit." Brad shrugged. "A recluse."

"A hermit?" Jonathan snorted loudly, his disgust evident.

A quiet, slightly garbled sound from Elise made Mitch turn, but Brad's words caught his attention instead.

"From what I've heard, Old Man Fogarty hasn't left his home since he bought it over ten years ago." Brad picked up a small rubber ball on his desk and tossed it into the air, catching it with ease. "So I don't think he'll be comin' into town. And, truth be told, he's exactly the kind of person who could disappear and no one would notice."

SHE HEARD MITCH running through the people they needed to interview. The reunion group members, the orienteering guys, and even Joe, but it wasn't sinking into her head. Her mind was on her uncle. A man she'd loved so deeply yet lost in the blink of an eye.

Elise looked across the room at Mitch, saw the way he moved around the station discussing strategy with Jonathan and Brad. He was so passionate about his profession, so determined to catch the bad guys. And as much as she wished it weren't so, she knew there was a chance he'd see Uncle Ken as one of those bad guys—someone who'd gotten away with another person's death.

How could she blame him if he did? *She* knew it was an accident, believed it with every fiber of her being. But she hadn't suffered the same kind of personal losses Mitch had.

Twisting her hands in her lap, Elise was sure of one thing. There was no way she could tell Mitch about Uncle Ken. She simply couldn't risk losing him. Sure, one day she'd have to—if their relationship progressed into a lasting one—but she'd cross that bridge when it came.

In the meantime, she couldn't ignore the relief she felt knowing that Uncle Ken was here on the island. He'd disappeared after the grand jury refused to indict him, retreated from the town that had turned on him at a time he needed support. Severed ties to everyone in the family, including her.

That loss of contact had weighed on her heart the past twelve years, crept into every fond memory she had of her time with him. *With them.*

Elise swiped at the tear that trickled down the side of her nose, willed herself to breathe slowly, to keep it together in front of Mitch.

She hadn't realized until that moment that her desire to come to Mackinac went way beyond cross country skiing and cuddling in front of a fireplace with Mitch. Somewhere in her subconscious she'd wanted to reconnect with a happy childhood moment. A moment in time when Uncle Ken and Aunt Faye were happy and full of plans for their future.

Elise shivered and looked out the window at the snow encrusted trees reaching toward the stationhouse like a pair of bony arms. Knowing that he had come here gave her hope that he, too, had been looking for the same connection.

Ten

4:00 p.m.

ELISE SLIPPED THE set of walkie talkies into her winter coat and waited as Mitch and Brad firmed up a meeting time for later in the evening.

It was hard not to feel a little hopeful now that plans were beginning to take shape. Jonathan had already headed back to his hotel with a set of walkie talkies; the other two sets would be used between Sophie's and The Island Inn. While certainly not a flawless system, the radios would enable Mitch and Brad to keep in touch with the places that housed the most people.

The skiers would be dispatched in the morning to round up the outlying residents, a group Elise planned to be a part of. She had to. It might be the only way to coax him out of that house.

"Elise?"

Looking up, she met Mitch's worried gaze. If she didn't watch her demeanor more closely, he was going to grow suspicious.

"Are you ready?" Elise forced her voice to sound natural, her lips to turn upward.

"Yeah. But you sure looked like you were a million miles away just now." She felt his leather clad fingers gently nudge her face upward so that she was, once again, looking into his eyes. "I'm gonna get us through this, Elise."

Tears sprang to her eyes as she looked at him. Tears of love for Mitch, tears of frustration for everything she wished she could share with him yet couldn't.

A burst of wind howled through the station as the front door banged open behind her.

Elise spun around and saw the anxious eyes that peered at her over the tightly wrapped red scarf.

"Can I help you?" Mitch asked.

The woman pulled her scarf down around her neck and pushed her hood back, revealing a long, dark blonde ponytail. "I'm not sure. I'm not sure if it's anything important. But I thought I should let Officer Matthews decide."

Brad put an arm on the woman's shoulder and guided her over to the lone chair in the station's waiting area. "Why don't you sit down and catch your breath a minute, Annie."

"I'm okay, I'll stand." The woman pulled her white woolen gloves from her hands and clenched them in her left fist. "I was working the front desk last night. It was a fairly busy night with many of our guests coming down, asking questions about the storm. The housekeeping crew stayed late and made sure everyone was comfortable and had something to eat."

Elise studied the woman as she spoke. It was hard not to rush her to the part that made her venture out in the snow to talk to Brad, but if she had learned anything over the past seven months at the newspaper, it was the simple fact that people share more if you simply shut up and listen.

"Anyway, last night around ten, a guy came in looking for a room. I didn't think much about it at the time. But today, I heard some of that ski group talking about their friend. You know, the one that was stabbed to death? That's when I started thinking." Annie dropped into the chair and looked at Mitch and Brad with big round eyes. "Who on earth would check into a hotel at ten o'clock in the middle of a blizzard when the last plane on the island was at two?"

Elise looked at Mitch, saw the way his eyebrows cocked as he squatted down beside the woman's chair.

"What can you tell us about this guy?"

"He was tall. His hair seemed to be dark, but it's hard to be certain. What wasn't tucked under his hat was covered with snow."

Elise covered her mouth with her hand and looked at Brad. His eyes were wide, his mouth slightly twisted. He too, seemed interested in the woman's account of the previous night's guest.

"Where do you work, Annie?" Mitch asked.

"The Lakeside Inn."

"That's Jonathan's hotel, isn't it?"

Brad and Elise nodded simultaneously.

"How do you know it was ten when this guy checked in?" The words surprised Elise as they escaped her mouth and she hoped Mitch and Brad wouldn't be angry. This was their interview—not hers.

"I know it had to be about ten because I'd had another guy come in at nine thirty asking for work. Poor thing was about my age and looked pathetically cold. He was wearing a flimsy coat with a blue blanket wrapped around his shoulders, a fairly full knapsack on his back, and an almost empty cup of coffee in his hand."

"A blue blanket?"

"Uh huh."

"That's gotta be the kid our sled driver told us about, Mitch." Elise pulled the small pad of paper Brad had given her from her pocket. "But if he arrived ahead of us, why'd it take him 'til almost ten to look for a room?"

"Good question!" Mitch said. "We need to find this kid and get some answers."

Elise turned back to Annie. "Did he say anything?" She could feel the reporter in her taking over, questions firing through her brain faster than she could ask them.

The woman shrugged. "He said he was here to see someone and was hoping to find a job. He wanted to know if I needed any help at the hotel in exchange for a room. I felt horrible telling him we weren't hiring. But he was real nice and said he understood. And then he left."

"And he ventured back out in the blizzard with nothing but that blanket?"

Annie lowered her voice and looked directly at Elise as she spoke. "Now I could get fired for this, but I gave him

58

another blanket from the housekeeping closet and refilled his coffee mug. I just didn't have the heart to send him out like that. Besides, he was kinda cute, ya know? Had a thick head of gorgeous wavy brown hair and blue eyes that just took your breath away."

"So how do you know the second guy came in at ten?" Mitch asked the woman gently.

"Because I looked at my watch 'bout the same time that cutie left and it was nine fifty-five. The other guy checked in 'bout five minutes later. Heck, they probably passed each other outside in the snow."

"Do you remember his name?"

"John. John Smith."

"That's original," Brad sneered.

"And obviously made up, which begs the obvious question—why?" Mitch ran his hand over his hair, and then placed it on the armrest of Annie's chair. "Could you ID him?"

Annie grew silent as she cast her eyes upward for a few short moments. "I only saw him for the time it took to get him a key and a travel item he forgot. He wasn't real chatty so it went pretty quick. But I think I could...if I saw him again."

Angry shouts outside the station interrupted any further questions. Elise looked out the window and saw a sled off the path, its driver yelling. Mitch and Brad pulled on their coats and hurried out the door, leaving the two women alone.

"Do you think I was an idiot for coming here?" Annie nervously tugged her hood upward, secured it to her head with a drawstring.

Elise touched the woman's shoulder. "Absolutely not. You did exactly the right thing."

A small smile temporarily erased the worry lines around Annie's eyes. "I best get back. The other desk guy and I are taking shifts since there's nowhere else to go and nothing else to do. This is my shift, but I asked one of the maids to cover for me so I could run over here real quick."

"Okay. Thanks, Annie, for all your help. I imagine we'll come up to your hotel as soon as the guys get that sled out. I'm sure Mitch is real anxious for you to ID this mystery guest."

"I'll be there. Ready to go." Annie slowly pulled her scarf over her mouth, then pulled it back down. "Hey, thanks for listening. And thanks for having that man bring over the walkie talkie."

"Jonathan gave it to you?"

"Yeah, I guess that was his name. I considered telling him about the guy last night, but decided not to. I've known Officer Matthews for a while now."

"You did fine, Annie. It's probably better that Brad and Mitch heard everything from your mouth anyway."

Elise followed Annie out the door and waved as the woman stepped off the porch and into shin-deep snow. The strength of the wind and the angle of the falling snow forced the hotel clerk to bend forward and cup her face with wool-covered hands.

She watched Annie walk for a few moments, then looked in the direction of the main road. It was completely deserted—the brutal weather forcing vacationers to view the island from behind a window. Cut off from everything. And everyone.

Eleven
4:40 p.m.

HE LOOKED AT the branches that sagged above him, weighed down by more than a foot of snow. His body was becoming numb to the cold, the tiny hairs in his nose stiff against his breath.

It would be nice to be somewhere warm for a while. But that would have to wait.

They'd left him no choice. He would have to deviate from his plan this one time. He simply couldn't risk being discovered until he was finished.

Twelve
4:40 p.m.

A SKIER IN a navy blue parka slid to a stop in front of the station and pulled his ski mask off.

Mark.

"Do they need more help?" he asked, pointing toward Mitch and Brad who were still working feverishly to get the old man's sled and horse out of the ditch.

Elise tried to smile, but it was hard. Mark was on Mitch's list of possible suspects. His best suspect in fact—until Annie came in. But she couldn't shake the nagging feeling that Mark was nothing more than a quiet, awkward guy.

"Yeah, I'm sure the guys will take all the help they can get right now. That horse is making it mighty hard on them."

Mark reached down, snapped off his skis and waded through the mounting snow. She stood on the front porch and watched, swirling flakes stinging her bare skin.

A few grunts later, the sled was out of the ditch and the horse was more than ready to be on its way.

Mitch, Brad and Mark walked back to the station door, brushing snow from their clothes.

"Thanks, Mark." Mitch pulled his wet glove off and extended his hand for the skier to shake.

"No problem."

"What brought you out in this?"

Elise studied Mitch, knew his innocent question held much more than simple conversation.

"I can't stop thinking about Pete. I know I just met the guy yesterday, but everyone's painted such a great picture of him. I guess it's bugging me that some creep killed him and is roaming the island. Free. Guess I'm kinda looking for him on my own."

Mitch hunched his shoulders and blew into his hands. He seemed to pause momentarily, ponder Mark's words.

"Well, we might have a lead. A hotel clerk at the Lakeside Inn checked someone in last night that may be of interest to us."

Elise stood transfixed to her spot, completely oblivious to the snow whipping around them. Why was Mitch sharing that kind of information with someone he suspected?

She glanced at Brad for his reaction and saw the same look of surprise on his face.

"In fact, she's in the station right now. Want to come in?" Mitch gestured toward the door, his eyebrow slightly cocked as he searched Mark's face.

"Um, Mitch. She. Left." Elise felt her stomach lurch. Mitch's question was pure bait. "She said she had to get back to work. I told her we'd be over soon."

The color drained from Mitch's face, as he pulled his gaze off Mark and stared at her. "You let her go?"

"Hey, no big deal. I gotta get going anyway. My feet are getting really cold." Mark reached down, snapped his skis into place, grabbed for the poles that rested against the station's brick exterior. "I'll see you around."

The threesome stood silently as they watched the parka-clad redhead ski off, his head bent low.

Mitch's low voice finally broke the silence.

"Crap."

Thirteen
5:20 p.m.

OH, WHAT SHE wouldn't do to turn the clock back an hour. That way she could actually use her brains and keep Annie at the station until Mitch and Brad finished digging out the sled. If she had done that, then Mitch would have been able to put his main suspect in front of the desk clerk right on the spot. Instead, Elise's rookie mistake caused him to tip his hand too early.

Elise jammed her hands deep into her coat pockets and trudged through the deepening snow behind Mitch and Brad.

"What's the odds that my damn snowmobile would pick now to run out of gas? I mean, how much more are we expected to take?"

Brad's frustration echoed in every biting word that left his mouth. Mitch and Brad couldn't be more different in the way they dealt with each roadblock thrown their way. While Brad whined and moaned, Mitch was silent.

She inhaled deeply, felt the cold air fill her lungs. As much as she wished they were somewhere, anywhere else at this very moment, she knew Mitch was needed here. Brad would have been useless to the island's residents if he'd had to go this alone.

"Here we are," Brad said. "The Lakeside Inn."

The Lakeside Inn was a quaint Victorian-style hotel that overlooked Lake Huron. The muted glow of kerosene escaped from several of the upper floor windows, a throwback to a long ago era that served as an unexpected blessing to hotel guests in this storm.

She was careful to avoid direct eye contact with Mitch as she walked through the door he held open. Even though he'd apologized for his reaction to Annie leaving the station, she still couldn't quite shake her own anger—at herself.

A single kerosene lantern atop the registration desk cast a shadowy light across the foyer. Small puddles of water pooled on the wood flooring beneath their feet, the warmth from the lobby fireplace beckoning them to come closer, dry off. The sitting area to the right of the desk was empty despite the much-needed heat provided by the crackling flames.

Elise set her elbow on the counter and looked around the tasteful room. The high-backed chairs and flowered upholstery were a perfect fit with the Victorian architecture.

It was hard not to wish for the trip this should have been, to wish for cozy evenings cuddled up with Mitch in front of a fire. But it wasn't meant to be.

Shaking her head against the useless images, Elise turned her gaze back to the desk area where she stood. A swivel chair sat empty, its exact color hard to pinpoint in the dimly lit room.

"Annie? Are you here?" She called out, her voice echoing in the empty room.

"Maybe she's with a guest." Brad walked toward the hearth, stopped briefly to rub his hands back and forth near the flames. "I imagine she's got her hands full with people who aren't used to a blizzard like this one. A lot of unsettled nerves. And that's without some of em' knowing what's really going on."

Elise looked back at the desk, at the empty chair, the turned-over waste basket, the assortment of pens scattered on the floor, and the long red scarf she hadn't noticed at first glance. She squinted in the lantern's pale light as her gaze traveled the path of the scarf.

"Elise?"

Somewhere in her subconscious she heard Mitch's voice, but her gaze, her attention, followed the scarf that stretched across the seat of the chair, a wide expanse of fabric that resembled a winding snake in search of its prey.

Leaning forward, Elise craned her neck to see over the countertop. A woman's shoe rested at the base of the chair.

She heard the scream escape her lips, tasted the bile that rose in her throat, felt the weakness in her legs as she gripped the counter for support.

Annie lie on the floor face down, the end of her red scarf knotted tightly around her neck.

ELISE KNEW SHE needed to stand up, to do whatever she could to help. But her stomach still felt so queasy, her legs rubbery.

Mitch and Brad were deep in conversation behind the desk, Annie's motionless body just inches from their feet. Elise shivered.

No matter what Mitch said, she couldn't shake the feeling of overwhelming guilt that flooded her being the instant she saw Annie.

Elise tightened her grip on the soggy wet tissue in her left hand and brushed it quickly across her eyes. Could she have done something different? Forced Annie to stay at the station until the guys had finished with the man's sled?

Maybe. Maybe not.

The sound of footsteps from the floor above echoed in her head, forced her thoughts away from Annie's decision and onto the other people in the hotel. Maybe someone had heard something, saw something.

But then again, no one had heard *her* scream when she saw the body. And Mitch and Brad were fairly certain that the tipped-over trash can and scattered pens meant Annie had struggled with her killer.

Elise pushed herself up off the chair and inhaled slowly, deeply. Sitting around wasn't going to bring Annie back.

She looked across the room, her gaze falling on the darkened computer screen to the right of the desk chair.

The computer.

"That's it!"

"Elise? You okay?"

Realizing she had spoken aloud, Elise clapped a hand over her mouth. But it was too late. She'd caught his attention.

Mitch was out from behind the desk and beside her before she could say another word. "Sit back down, Elise. We'll take care of this."

She felt his warm fingers under her chin, the gentle upward nudge of her face until her eyes finally met his.

"Elise?"

"I'm okay, Mitch. I just can't sit here anymore. I've got to do something. And the computer gave me an idea."

"Computer?"

"The one behind the desk. They must keep a record of all guests who check in and the rooms that they are given."

Mitch's gaze left her face and moved across the room to the computer. "There's no power, Elise."

"I know. But they still had to keep track someway."

Mitch exhaled loudly and clapped his hands together. "Oh man, that's great. Do you feel up to looking?"

Elise reached out and touched Mitch's right hand. "Yeah, I do. I can't sit back any longer."

"Okay, then let's get to work." Mitch kissed her on the top of her head, whispered in her ear. "We'll be okay."

"I know."

Elise headed for the desk area, Mitch in tow. As she rounded the corner she forced her eyes away from Annie's body and onto the computer. This particular area was still neat and orderly with only the essentials in sight of the guests.

The shadow of a flashlight to the left of the computer caught her eye, and it didn't take long to figure out why Annie had kept one there. This area of the clerk's desk received little light from the kerosene lamp on the registration counter, making it almost impossible to see anything—let alone read or write.

She reached for the flashlight and switched it on, moved the beam around. A large wicker basket, filled with assorted travel-sized hygiene items, sat to the left of where the flashlight had been. Most of the basket's items were arranged neatly in groups of four; four soaps, four shampoos, four toothbrushes, four conditioners, four razors, three bottles of shaving cream.

Elise moved the flashlight to the right, its beam illuminating two lone objects on the blotter beside the keyboard. The first item was a folder of guest invoices, the second a small brown notebook with a single word across the cover.

Guests.

Eagerly, she flipped it open.

"What're you guys doing back there?"

Elise instinctively shut the book. A shadowy figure stood on the other side of the counter.

Brad's greeting identified the man.

"Aw man, Jonathan, you scared the crap out of us."

Elise walked over to where Mitch and Brad stood, resisted the urge to look down at Annie.

"What's going on?"

Mitch jerked his head in the direction of the stairs and then spoke quietly, careful to keep his voice from being heard by anyone other than the four of them.

"We've got another body."

The light from the kerosene lamp captured the surprise on Jonathan's face. "Who? Where?"

Mitch stepped back and pointed downward. "The desk clerk."

Jonathan was behind the desk in an instant, kneeling beside Annie's body. "I just talked to her when I came back from the station. I showed her how to use the walkie talkie if she needed anything." His voice trailed off as he shook his head in disbelief. "Why didn't she call for help?"

Mitch shrugged. "She came to the station after you left this afternoon. Said she checked someone in last night. Hours after the last plane arrived. After the power went out. Said she could ID him for us."

Mitch ran his hand across his eyes and over his hair before continuing. "She headed back over here while we helped some guy get his sled out of a snow bank. But by the time we got over here to find out who this mystery guest is, she was dead."

Jonathan's voice, quiet but steady, confirmed what Elise already knew to be true. "He must have known she could ID him."

It was hard not to cringe as she listened to Mitch fill Jonathan in on the happenings at the police station after he'd left. When Mitch got to the part about Mark, Elise stared at the floor. At Annie.

There was no doubt that Mark was quiet, even a little aloof, but she'd bet her last dollar that he wasn't the killer.

Jonathan rose to his feet and looked at Elise. "You okay, hon?"

Elise nodded slowly. "I'm hoping I can find something in these records that'll help us out." She motioned to the computer area.

Jonathan cleared his throat, turned toward Mitch and Brad.

"You guys okay to take care of the body?"

"Yeah." Mitch's confident tone was a stark contrast to the uncertainty in Brad's face.

"Okay then. I'll go through guest records with Elise and see if we can't find something that will tell us who this mystery guest is."

Elise led Jonathan to the computer area and picked up the flashlight once again. Its large circular beam shone down on the invoice folder and the guest notebook.

She flipped the book open, ran a trembling finger down the names assigned to each room as Jonathan searched the desk. A few of the guys from the orienteering group were on the list, names Elise recognized from listening to Sophie at the restaurant during the search for Pete Garner. Drew Riker, Josh Cummings, Mark Tallberg...

"Mark!"

Elise stared at the book, her mind reeling. Once again, everything came back to the burly redhead. Maybe Mitch was right.

"Well, well, well, would you look at that. Hey, Mitch, Brad. Come here." Jonathan raised his hand in the air and motioned to the men. "Three guesses on who shows up in the guest book."

Jonathan took the small brown notebook from Elise's grip and placed it in Mitch's outstretched hand.

Elise shined the flashlight above the notebook and waited as Mitch read the list of names aloud.

"Jim and Carrie Sanders, Drew Riker, Josh Cummings, Luke and Sasha Meeton, Mark Tallberg." Mitch whistled under his breath and shook his head. "He's like a bad penny that keeps turning up, isn't he?"

"Should we go get him?" Brad shifted from foot to foot, his voice increasing in pitch with each word he spoke. "Let's pull him in and put an end to this now."

"You can't do that," Elise said. "He's quiet. That's all you've got. That's not a crime."

She could hardly believe the words that tumbled from her mouth, but she couldn't stop them once they started.

"What about the reunion group? And Mark's name is too far down the page to be the man who checked in last night. We should be focused on *this* name." Elise moved her index finger to the last name in the guest book.

John Smith.

Just like Annie said.

"Elise is right." Mitch leaned against the desk and studied the guest book. "Most likely John Smith is a fake name, but its position in the book does take the focus off Mark a little."

Elise studied Mitch's face closely, recognized the familiar look creeping across it. A look that meant he had a plan.

"This is something we definitely need to look into. But I still say it doesn't hurt to watch Mark. Closely. And who better to do that than you, Jonathan."

"Me? Why?"

"Because you're staying here too and he doesn't know you're a cop."

Jonathan's head bobbed slowly, a slight smile tugged at the corners of his mouth. "Makes sense. Consider me on the job."

"Then you probably shouldn't be back here with us in case he walks into the lobby." Elise spoke quietly, hoped she wasn't overstepping.

"She's right, Jonathan. You better head out of here." Mitch stepped backward and began to search the shelves under the registration desk. "Where do you think Annie put the walkie talkie you gave her?"

"Right here." Jonathan grabbed a small rectangular object from beside the wicker basket and held it up for everyone to see. "I just hope it helps us more than it helped her."

"Hey! What's going on here?"

The foursome turned simultaneously and stared at the young man who stood before them, hands on hips, a look of irritation on his face.

"Hey, Tom. It's okay." Brad stepped forward into the lantern's light. "It's me. Brad."

"Oh, hey, sorry about that Brad. What are you doing back here? And who are they?" The young man motioned at the rest of them. "Where the heck is Annie? She knows she's supposed to be on desk duty."

"Tom, this is my friend Detective Mitch Burns." Brad pointed at Mitch, then pointed at Elise. "This is Elise Jenkins. And that's Jonathan Moore—but you probably know him by now."

"I've only seen Annie since I've been here." Jonathan said quietly. "I guess my comings and goings haven't coincided with Tom's shift."

The desk clerk exhaled loudly through clenched teeth, tapped his foot on the wood floor. "Where the hell is Annie? I swear this is not my day. My damn snowmobile was out of gas, so I ended up having to hoof it back here in the snow. And now Annie's not here. She's not supposed to leave until she's covered."

"Your snowmobile was out of gas?" Mitch's words were terse, angry.

"Yeah." Tom nodded, his eyes wide, yet tired. "It's the strangest thing, too. I thought I had a full tank of gas when I left. But no siree. The stupid needle on the gas gage must be frozen along with everything else."

Elise could feel the tension coming from Mitch as the pieces of the puzzle began to fall into place. Brad had sworn he'd had a full tank, too. Was it a coincidence? Or was the killer tampering with their only form of real transportation?

"Look, I don't mean to be rude, but where's Annie?" Tom asked again. "Why are you guys behind the desk?"

Brad looked at Mitch and shrugged. Elise felt sorry for Brad. It was obvious he had come to this island to pursue a career he'd probably dreamt of since he was a boy, yet really wasn't cut out to do. And now, the safety of so many was in his hands. A responsibility he was more than willing to push onto Mitch.

She shifted foot to foot as Mitch took hold of Tom's shoulder and guided him to a quiet corner of the lobby where they could talk in peace. Peace that would be shattered, once again, as another innocent person learned of the fate closing in on all of them.

"You okay, Elise?"

Why was it that everyone seemed to feel as if Mitch would make things right? That Mitch would fix everything and make it better? Why didn't anyone ever worry about him?

"Elise?"

Her eyes lingered on Mitch, now sitting in a tiny corner of the lobby with Tom and Brad, his mouth moving as he undoubtedly told the young clerk about Annie's tragic death.

"Elise?"

She forced her attention onto Jonathan's tall form, the silver walkie talkie in his hand.

The walkie talkie.

"Elise, are you okay?"

"Huh?" She shook her head against the vague but troubling thoughts that seemed to rise just to the surface before slipping deep into her subconscious. "What did you say?"

"I asked if you're okay. You seem like you're on another planet right now."

"I wish I was."

She felt Jonathan's gentle squeeze on her shoulder.

"This will all be over soon. You'll see." He slipped the walkie talkie into his pocket. "Tell Mitch I'm heading out before Mark shows up. I'll check in with you guys soon."

She smiled faintly and nodded as Jonathan headed into the shadows of the lobby and disappeared up the staircase.

ELISE PEERED AROUND the tiny registration area one last time, her eyes lingering on the guest book beside the invoice folder. What was it that was bothering her so much? Everything was exactly as it had been when she began her search, so what was the problem?

She moved the swivel chair into place under the computer monitor, her thoughts replaying the events of the past hour. Tom had taken the news of Annie's death fairly well. Sure, he'd been rattled, but he seemed to have a little bit of Mitch's spirit—the kind that faced adversity head on. He'd even shown Mitch a few of the karate moves he knew in case someone tried to attack him.

She hated the thought that Mitch, Brad, and Tom were temporarily burying Annie under the snow behind the hotel. But it made sense. The cold snow would provide a refrigeration effect, which was the best they could do until the blizzard was over. Still, she couldn't wait for them to be done.

Her fingers brushed lightly across the cover of the guest book, her eyes lingered once again on the invoice folder and wicker basket filled with travel items. What was it that was nagging her thoughts?

A thump on the registration desk made her turn. Mark's scowling face was barely visible in the dim light from the lantern.

"What do I need to do to get a safe around—?"

He stopped speaking as a spark of recognition flashed across his face.

"What are *you* doing here?"

Elise felt her mouth drop open, her cheeks redden.

Her heart leapt in her chest as the door off the back hallway clicked and the sound of footsteps headed in their direction.

Gratefully, she turned and waited for Mitch to emerge from the tiny hallway that linked the registration desk to the back door.

"She should be okay there until this damn storm lets up and we can give her a proper bur—"

The second Mitch stepped through the door Elise jerked her eyes in the direction of Mark. His jaw tightened and a protective arm slid around her waist.

"Hey, Mark. What's up?"

"I was just asking your girlfriend here that same question. I can't help but feel like you guys have an issue with me."

"What makes you say that?" Mitch asked.

"You're always staring at me. During the search, at Sophie's, after I helped get that sled out of the ditch, now."

"Sorry you feel that way, Mark."

"If you've got a problem, spit it out. If not, leave me alone." Mark's scowl deepened as he looked from Mitch, to Brad, to Elise, and back again. Finally, he waved his hand in the air. "Where's the desk clerk?"

Tom stepped forward. "What can I do for you, sir?"

"I need a safe."

"Right away, sir. We've got several here behind the desk."

Mark looked back at Mitch and leaned forward on the counter. "If you guys are wanting something to do while you try to figure out who killed Pete, maybe you should take care of some other police business."

"Meaning?"

"Meaning, I could use a little protection from that idiot, Josh."

"Josh Cummings?" Mitch crossed his arms in front of his chest and stared at Mark.

"Yeah. From the orienteering club. I caught the bastard trying to get into my room."

Tom stepped forward, grabbed for the pen and paper on the counter. "What would he want in your room, sir?"

"My prize money, that's what."

Fourteen
8:00 p.m.

ELISE TOSSED HER notepad onto the coffee table and inched forward on the sofa. The firelight provided enough illumination to see Mark's face, but fell short in its role as a reading lamp.

But it didn't matter. The questions were on the tip of her tongue, waiting to shoot from her mouth at the appropriate times.

"Can I ask when you arrived on the island?"

Mark tented his fingers, his elbows planted on the armrests of the single high-backed chair. She was glad to see his features had softened somewhat since Tom put his prize money in the hotel safe.

"I arrived last Sunday," he answered.

"What brought you here?"

"I didn't take much of my vacation time last year on account of the wild fires out west. The department gave us a grace period in carrying them over, but we needed to use 'em or lose 'em."

Elise nodded. "You're a firefighter?"

"Yup."

"For how long?"

Mark blew against his fingertips, rolled his eyes upward. "It'll be eleven—wait, no. It'll be twelve years in March."

She tapped the pen cap on her leg as she did some quick math. If she was accurate, Mark would be about 32 years old.

"I'm 31."

Her mouth dropped open and she stared at the redhead who sat across from her. "How'd you know I was gonna ask that?"

"You had that math face."

"Math face?"

"You're a writer. You work with the opposite side of your brain. People who are math oriented don't even have to think about numbers, it's just there. I could almost see your wheels turning. In fact, if the room wasn't so shadowed, I'd be willing to bet your fingers were moving."

It felt good to laugh, to release some of the tension she'd felt since Mitch assigned her Mark's interview.

"Touché."

Now that she'd had time to process everything, it made perfect sense that Mitch had let her have Mark. Her mind was still open where the redhead was concerned.

"So, what made you pick this island?"

"I used to cross country ski with my grandfather when I was a kid. Loved it." Mark dropped his hands to his thighs and leaned back in his chair. "I'd read about this place in a magazine at the firehouse one day. Figured it would be perfect for sneaking in some skiing and having some quiet time for myself."

"Sucker." She reached for one of the sodas Tom had left out for them, peered at Mark's face as she lifted the metal tab and raised the can to her lips.

He laughed a deep sound that filled their tiny alcove. "Yeah, I guess I kinda am. This place certainly hasn't been the stuff tourist brochures are made of, has it?"

"No. But I happen to know this island is amazing under normal circumstances."

"You've been here before?"

"A long, long time ago." She could hear the wistful tone to her voice, was grateful when Mark heeded the sound and allowed her to resume the role of interviewer.

"Is there anything you remember from the morning of the competition that could help us? A person walking in the woods? A scream? Anything?"

Mark leaned forward, reached for a can of soda.

"I've thought about that morning over and over since we found Pete. I don't remember seeing anything out of the ordinary."

Elise nodded slowly, her gaze locked on the flames in the hearth as she considered her next question.

"But the guy who did this must have been a force to contend with."

Elise looked at Mark. "Why do you say that?"

"Because I saw Pete as he was finding his ninth point and he was focused on that finish line. You know, eye of the tiger focused."

"You saw him after the competition started?"

Mark nodded, crushed the now-empty can against his thigh. "Yup. I had just found my eighth point and was sure I was winning. Even toyed with him a little about the legendary winning streak everyone had talked about that morning."

"How did he respond to you?"

"Like any cocky jock would. With a spark in his eye and the promise of my defeat."

Elise looked across the room and saw Mitch huddled in another corner talking to Drew and Josh. Was this information he'd want to hear firsthand?

"It didn't bother me if that's what you're thinking."

She turned, her focus on Mark once again.

"It didn't?"

"No. I'm a competitor, too. Sure, I wanted to be the guy who showed up out of nowhere and won, but I respected his determination." Mark raised the crushed can to eye level and threw it into a nearby trashcan with disgust. "I sure as hell didn't want to win the way I did."

There wasn't much she could say to that. He was right. Who would want to win a prize simply because the true winner had been murdered?

"Why are you so certain that Josh Cummings is after your money?" she finally asked.

Even as the question left her mouth she could see the tension resurfacing in Mark's features. His jaw muscles tightened, his eyes narrowed.

"He is the epitome of a sore loser. He screamed like a spoiled brat when I won that money, accused me of cheating." Mark rose to his feet. "And if there is one thing people can bank on about me, it's the fact that I don't cheat. Ever."

"So let's go over this one more time," Mitch said. He looked from Drew to Josh, and back again. Both men still seemed so affected by Pete's fate. And he couldn't blame them. They'd lost a friend. "Even though he'd had heart trouble in the past, he still managed to win the competitions each time, right?"

Drew nodded, his hand cupped over his mouth.

"What made him so good?" Mitch gently prodded.

Dropping his hand to his lap, Drew started to speak, then stopped.

"It's okay. I know this is hard."

"He was driven."

Mitch felt his eyebrows arch as Drew's choice of words settled in his thoughts.

"How do you mean?"

"Pete had essentially been told by his cardiologist that he better get in shape if he wanted to be around when it was time to be a grandpa. And like any true athlete would, he heard that warning as a starter pistol. He set his mind to finding a form of exercise that he'd enjoy."

"And orienteering was it?"

"Yup. He read about our group in the paper one day. He'd always loved being outdoors and was somewhat of a map geek from what I gathered in our early conversations. He came to one of our events and was hooked."

"How soon did he start winning?"

"About as fast as my soon-to-be ex spent my paycheck," Josh interjected.

Mitch focused his gaze on the short, squatty guy Dan Friar had pointed out to him just yesterday morning. "Did that bother you?"

Josh raised his palms into the air and rapidly moved them back and forth. "Not me. I could have whipped his butt if I'd wanted to."

Drew snorted and turned his head in Josh's direction. "Not likely."

"Ah c'mon, Drew. We both know he won 'cuz he had a better compass than the rest of us."

Drew smacked his fist onto the armrest of his chair. "Don't even go there! Pete had just gotten that damn compass a few weeks ago, and he'd been winning for years."

Mitch studied the men as they argued. It was obvious to him that Drew wasn't going to let a loser like Josh sully Pete's accomplishments.

"I'd have won with that compass."

"Don't make me laugh. You've been arguing with compasses and maps for two years. *That's* why you lose, Josh. You've got no common sense."

Sensing the direction the interview was headed, Mitch took hold of the reins once again.

"Josh, I understand that you were, um, how shall I say this? A little pissed off when Mark won. Is that accurate?"

"Try having your wife drag you through the court system. It ain't cheap. I needed that damn money." Josh jumped to his feet and started pacing, his hands clenching and unclenching. "I was sure I was in the lead this time. But noooo, that damn redheaded guy had to show up. There is no doubt in my mind he cheated somehow."

"And why would you think this competition was any different than all the others?" Drew asked, his voice dripping with irritation. "You lost all of those, too."

"My luck was changing. I could feel it. I finally had what I needed to win."

"Hatred for your wife?" Drew shot back.

"No, but that certainly didn't hurt."

Mitch walked over to the registration desk, his thoughts still on the conversation with Drew and Josh. Nothing they'd said seemed to point to the killer, but then again, he knew all too well how the most insignificant things could sometimes be the dynamite that blew a case wide open.

He stopped beside Elise and slid his arm around her waist.

"How'd it go with Mark?"

"I think he's clean. I really do. In fact, I kinda like him. He actually has a good sense of humor," Elise said. "He willingly answered every question I threw at him, volunteering information I didn't even ask for."

"Okay." He turned toward Brad. "And the reunion folks?"

"They're all accounted for. They've been here for a week and nobody new has shown up since the day they all arrived." Brad plucked an apple from the fruit bowl on the registration desk. "This group has its share of former prom queens, chess players, and jocks. Just no serial killers."

Mitch raised his arms above his head and stretched. "You got your walkie talkie, Tom?"

"Sure do." The desk clerk held the piece of equipment up and grinned. "I'll be fine. I'm almost a black belt, remember?"

Mitch grinned, patted the countertop quickly. "I remember. But if you need anything, call Jonathan, okay?"

"Where you guys headed?"

"Elise and I are headed to our hotel. We need some sleep. We've got skiers heading out at daybreak to bring in the outlying residents." Mitch rubbed his palm across his stubbled chin. "You ready to house a few of them for us?"

"Sure thing. We got plenty of room."

"What are you gonna do, Brad?" Mitch asked, looking at his buddy.

"I'm gonna go sack out at the station."

"Are you sure?"

"Yeah, I feel better with guns nearby."

Saturday, January 29th
Fifteen
8:30 a.m.

SHE COULD TELL Mitch didn't understand. And in a way she couldn't blame him. It made no sense why she'd be so hell-bent on being part of the group assigned to round up the outlying residents. No sense to him, anyway.

But to Elise, it made perfect sense. If there was any chance of coaxing her uncle out of that house, it would have to come from her. And even that was slim.

She looked down, tugged the insulated glove up further on her wrist. It had been nearly fourteen years since she'd seen him. Even after all this time it was hard to picture that quiet, gentle man confined to a house in the middle of nowhere for over a decade. A confinement that was apparently his self-imposed punishment for an accident he never meant to happen.

Sure, she'd dreamed of finding him one day. But as time passed, and no contact was ever made, her hope for that "someday" had all but faded away. In fact, if not for Brad's confirmation on the night she and Mitch arrived, she'd still wonder if he were even alive anymore.

"Is there anything I can do to talk you out of this?"

Elise looked up, met Mitch's uncertain eyes. "No. I'm a good skier, Mitch. This is something I can do to help."

She prayed that he would understand her need to do this, but knew full well that he didn't, couldn't. He didn't know about her uncle's presence on the island. And it needed to stay that way. If there was one thing she knew about Mitch

Burns, it was the fact that he believed in justice and had zero tolerance for those who didn't face the consequences for their actions. It still ate away at him the way his father's killer eluded prison because of a mental incompetence. So there was no reason to think he'd look at Aunt Faye's death and the grand jury's failure to indict Uncle Ken any different than everyone else. And if he knew where she stood on the whole subject it might be enough to send him packing.

Mitch reached out and brushed a fine layer of snow from her parka as they stood outside Sophie's restaurant. "I don't understand this, Elise. I really don't. But I'll respect your need to do this under one condition."

Elise pulled her hat down over her ears, knotted the bright plaid scarf around her neck. "What's that?"

"You stick with Dan and Drew. They're strong guys. Don't go heading off down a path or to a house unless those two are right by your side. Okay?"

She nodded and managed a smile as she reached out and squeezed his hand. The concern in his face and words was touching, reassuring.

"Ready to go, Elise?"

She turned and saw Dan Friar as he stepped out of Sophie's Place and grabbed his skis.

"Yes."

"You got the walkie talkie right, Dan?" Mitch asked.

"Sure do."

"I think this island is small enough that we'll be able to keep in touch for at least some of the area you'll be covering. But don't take any unnecessary risks. If someone is adamant that they want to stay in their house, then let it go. There is only so much we can do."

"Got it, Mitch. And don't worry, we'll keep her safe."

"I'm counting on that."

Elise glanced back over her shoulder at Mitch. She saw his body sag as the group set off toward the most isolated sections of the island.

The livery on the northern side of the island was old and rundown. Patches of rotted wood were visible just above the line of snow that rose roughly two feet up the building. A cockeyed sign, hung above the stable doorway, held two faded words—Stodder's Livery.

The sound of a horse's exhale escaped through the open walkway between stalls and brought a sense of life to the otherwise quiet stable. Elise pulled the glove from her right hand and reached between the steel bars of the stall. The horse's skin felt cold beneath her fingers, but the animal's eyes were warm and gentle.

She peered around the roomy stall as she patted the horse. She was pleased at the ample supply of food and water nearby. It was easy to see that the dilapidated building did not reflect the care the horses received.

"Who's there?"

Elise spun around and saw the elderly man staring at them from behind the barrel of a shotgun.

"Hey, man, it's okay." Dan's hands rose in the air as he spoke slowly, soothingly, to the balding man blocking the doorway. "Officer Matthews asked us to come out and check on you."

"Why?"

"Because this storm's knocked out power and phone lines everywhere and Brad wants to make sure you're okay." Elise heard the fear in Dan's voice as he waited for the man to lower his gun, a fear that she remembered all too well.

"So? We've had storms like this before."

"Please, put down the gun. We're not here to hurt you." Dan slowly lowered his hands as he spoke. "There's been two murders on the island in the past two days and Brad sent us out to check on all of the outlying residents. We're hoping you'll come back with us and stay in one of the hotels until this storm is over."

The man lowered the gun a smidge and pointed at Elise. "Why'd they send you?"

She willed her breathing to slow, her stance to soften. "I volunteered. We're all pitching in, in whatever way we can. And I'm a strong skier."

The man studied them for several long minutes then finally released his grip on the rifle. "I'm sorry about this. You just can't ever be too cautious these days. My brother lives over on the mainland and he had two of his horses stolen right outta his barn last month. And I knew that most sane people wouldn't be looking for no pony rides in this storm." He stepped forward, held out his hand. "I'm Vic. Vic Stodder. I own this place."

Elise turned toward Dan and Drew, noticed the way their bodies slumped with relief. There was nothing like staring at the end of a gun to send a jolt of terror through your body.

"What do you say? Will you come back with us?" Dan shook the man's outstretched hand.

"Nah, can't do that. I gotta make sure the new kid is taking care of my horses right."

"But sir, it's dangerous for you to be out here away from everyone. A place like this is a perfect place for someone looking to hide." Drew gestured to the horses. "We could help you hitch them to a sled or wagon and get them into town, too."

The man began to shake his head before Drew was finished talking. "No can do. I got me too many horses to hitch to one—or even three sleds, and this snow is too damn deep for them anyway. Besides, I got my own protection." He patted the rifle he'd finally leaned against the wall. "Ain't no one gonna be bothering me."

Elise looked around the stable slowly. "You said you have a new worker?"

"Yup. That's right. Name's R.J. He's 'bout your age, I imagine. Well, maybe not quite. He's probably a few years younger than you. Showed up Thursday night looking for work. Said he was good with horses. So I gave him a shot."

"Where is he now?"

"Sleeping. I'm giving him a place to put his head in exchange for work." Vic Stodder motioned to a stall on the far right of the stable. "Lilly Belle over there ain't been feeling real well. She's due any time now. R.J.'s coming when he did has been a real blessing."

Elise walked over to Lilly Belle's stable and peered through the bars. The horse stood still, her breath slow and labored. "Did R.J. say why he was here?"

"He said he's here to reconnect with someone, but asked me to respect his privacy. So I am. But why all these questions about R.J.?"

Elise turned. "We don't know who he is."

Vic Stodder waved his hand in the air and snorted. "He ain't no criminal if that's what you're implying. That kid has a heart of gold the way he cared for Lilly Belle last night. And he ain't got no money so he can't be no thief. Heck, all he had when he got here was a knapsack, an empty mug, and two blankets wrapped around him."

Elise's stomach tightened as Vic continued.

"And it's working out great. He's been here less than forty-eight hours and I tell ya, he's got a real knack with them horses. He's been just what I was looking for."

She reached for Dan's arm and squeezed it, her gaze still focused on Vic. "Are you sure we can't convince you to come with us, Mr. Stodder?"

"I'm sure. I'll be just fine." The man picked up his rifle and nodded. "Ain't no one gonna mess with me and my horses."

Elise managed a wan smile and wave at Vic Stodder as she tugged Dan towards the door.

"We need to check in with Mitch. Now."

She was grateful Dan waited to respond until the threesome was safely away from the stable.

"What's wrong, Elise?"

"That kid. R.J. He's one of the guys who showed up at the Lakeside Inn on Thursday night. One of the guys the last victim mentioned. We need to let Mitch and Brad know so that they can question him."

Dan whistled low under his breath, pulled the walkie talkie from his pocket and pressed the button.

"Mitch, do you read me? Mitch?"

The lack of familiar static brought a sinking feeling to her heart, a feeling that was confirmed by Drew.

"Sounds like we're out of range."

"Damn it." Dan shoved the walkie talkie back into the pocket of his parka and snapped his skis onto his feet. "C'mon, let's head back."

Elise stared at Dan and Drew. "We can't! We need to meet up with the rest of the skiers. We need to hit that cabin over by the airport."

"No we don't. I sent the rest of the team over to that place while we checked out the livery. We'll meet up with them in town."

Tears sprung to her eyes as she watched Dan's back glide toward the pathway in front of Vic Stodder's property. There was no way she was going to be able to convince him to head toward her uncle's house now. In his mind it was being taken care of.

"Elise?"

She turned and looked at Drew as he waited for her to follow. Clenching her hands, she willed herself to move forward. Time was wasting away as she stood there, torn between what her heart wanted and what her head knew had to be done.

Wrapping her hands around the poles, Elise pushed off the snow and followed Dan. She knew what the other skiers would say about their efforts to convince "the hermit" to stay in town until the storm was over.

And she knew what she would have to do in response.

She would simply have to find a way to get back to that cabin. Alone.

Sixteen
10:45 a.m.

MITCH USED TO love snow. Loved the way it slowed everyone down, the way it coated the bare tree branches and glistened in the sun, the way it drew people outdoors and made you feel like a kid again.

But this snow was different. Very different. This snow made people stay indoors, locked inside and huddled by a fireplace waiting for the power to return and the snow to stop falling.

In fact, the snow had become a sort of jail cell for everyone on the island. Everyone except the psychopath who was out there, somewhere. Waiting. For him the snow meant freedom.

Mitch exhaled slowly and strained to make out any sign of movement, any indication that Elise and the other skiers were on their way back. But the long, narrow pathway that ran in front of all the hotels and businesses in this section remained empty. No sign of life anywhere.

"Mitch, why don't you come away from that window for awhile and have some coffee. Your Elise will be back soon, I'm sure of it."

He looked down the road toward the woods one last time, squinted in an effort to see further. But there was nothing.

"Ah, Sophie, where are they?" He turned from the window as he spoke, met Sophie's troubled eyes with his own.

"They've been gone for over two hours and this island isn't that big. And I haven't heard from them in over an hour."

Sophie's hand felt warm on his wrist as she pulled him towards a nearby table.

"No, the island isn't that big. But you have to remember that this storm—and the snow we already have—is going to slow them down." She smiled at him. "And just because they're on skis doesn't mean they can go Mach-two with their hair on fire.

"And besides, you don't know some of these old-timers around here like I do. They can be mighty S-T-U-B-B-O-R-N and set in their ways. Getting them to move into town, even with news of danger, isn't gonna sit well with some of them. I tell you, Elise and those men have their work cut out for them this morning."

It was pretty much the same thing Brad had said when Mitch left him at the station thirty minutes ago to head back to Sophie's to wait.

"I guess I'm just mad at myself for being such an imbecile and not knowing how to ski."

Sophie shook her head, the corners of her mouth inching upward. "Not knowing how to ski does not make you an imbecile, Detective. It simply means you didn't grow up around it. Be honest, how much snow do you really get in southern New Jersey anyway? Enough to make a snowman once a year?"

She was right and he knew it. But if he'd known how to ski he could have gone with the group. With Elise. But then again, he wasn't too sure Elise had even wanted him to come. Her eyes had seemed so vacant that morning, so distant. And if he was honest with himself, she'd been like that since they got here.

"I've got a pot of coffee on the propane stove and it should be just about ready by now. Wait right here."

"Thanks, Sophie." He looked up from the table and forced a smile to his lips. Sophie was a sweet lady, she really was.

He watched the woman disappear through the swinging doorway behind the register. Coffee would be good, would help clear his thoughts. Help him focus.

It was odd how a simple plinking of cups and saucers in the distance could bring a sense of normalcy to an otherwise chaotic setting. But, odd or not, he allowed the momentary reprieve to relax his shoulders as he looked around the empty restaurant. The picture-covered walls were such a neat idea. Photographs were fun to look at even if you didn't know the people smiling back.

He sought out the table where he and Elise had sat less than forty-eight hours earlier. The same table where they had sat and laughed about the possibility of being snowed in and forced to extend their vacation. Little did they know the storm, and their vacation, held very different plans than the ones they'd envisioned.

"Here you go, Mitch."

"Thanks, Sophie." He reached for the large mug of black coffee she'd placed on the table and took a long, slow sip.

The diminutive woman sat across from him, her eyes tired and sad. "I heard about Annie."

"You did?"

Sophie nodded. "Tom came in here for a thermos of coffee this morning on his way back to work at the hotel. I could tell he was upset. I guess you could say I pulled it out of him."

He exhaled slowly, ran his forefinger around the rim of the mug. "I wish I could say it wasn't true, but I can't."

"Things are bad, aren't they?"

Mitch raised the mug to his mouth, took another long sip of the steaming black liquid. "Yeah. They are." He reached across the table, patted Sophie's cold hand. "But we're gonna figure this out, I promise you that."

Sophie's mouth turned upward, her midnight blue eyes sparkled momentarily. "I thank God that Brad's got you and the other police officer. I'm not sure he could handle this without you guys."

He pulled his hand back to the mug, gripped the warm porcelain with his hand. "I think Brad would've been fine. He's a good guy. But having Jonathan is definitely a Godsend as my Aunt Betty would say."

Mitch took another sip of coffee then glanced down at his watch.

"She'll be here soon, Mitch."

"Am I that transparent?"

"You're in love." Sophie straightened her apron across her lap. "I like Elise, she's a sweet girl. I enjoyed her company very much when you guys were out searching for that missing skier yesterday morning. And she sure seems to be smitten by you."

Mitch set the cup down, ran his right hand across his eyes and over his hair. "Elise is the best. She really is. I just hope you're right about the last part."

Sophie leaned forward, against the table. "You can't be serious. You've got to know she's crazy about you."

"Yeah, I'm serious. I sensed something with her when we were in the sled on the way to the hotel that first afternoon, but didn't really think much about it at the time." He slid his hand between the mug and the handle and slumped in his chair. "Then today she insisted on being part of the group to go out and round up the residents. And I mean *insisted*. I can't help but feel it was a way to get away from me for awhile."

Sophie reached across the table and touched his wrist.

"Mitch, this whole thing has to be very frightening for her. It's frightening for all of us."

He focused on the steam that rose from his mug. "I know. And it's gotta be hitting some raw nerves for Elise. This isn't the first time she's been in a situation like this. And last time she almost lost her life."

"Good heavens, Mitch. What happened?" The concern in the woman's voice made his head snap up. And in that instant, he understood why he was sharing so much with a woman he barely knew. Sophie reminded him of Aunt Betty.

"It's a long story, Sophie. But there was a case I was working on last summer that involved four murder victims. Elise came very close to being number five."

The woman pulled her hand from the table and shivered.

"It's okay, Sophie. It's actually the reason we came here. Elise came into some reward money after that and she wanted to take a trip. To get away." The words sounded so cruel, so ironic to his own ears.

Some getaway.

"Then, Mitch, you have to know that anything you're picking up from her right now has nothing to do with you. Her vacation has turned into an unexpected and unwanted trip down memory lane."

Maybe Sophie was right. But still, he couldn't shake the nagging feeling that something else was going on with Elise.

"It's such a shame, too, because I think she really would've loved it here," Sophie continued. "It's such a peaceful place no matter what season."

"That's just it. She *did* love it here. It's why she wanted to come back."

"Come back?"

"Yeah. She was here once as a kid. With her aunt and uncle. She said it was the best vacation she'd ever had."

Sophie leaned forward once more. "When was that?"

"Oh, I don't know. I think she said she was nine, so that would be about fourteen years ago."

"I bet her aunt and uncle are touched that this place holds such pleasant memories for her."

Mitch picked up his cup and drained the last few drops of coffee into his mouth. "You'd think. But her aunt died in some sort of an accident a year or so later and Elise lost touch with her uncle after that."

He set the empty mug on the table and pushed back his chair. "Well, you won, Sophie. I stopped staring out the window for awhile. But the suspense is killing me. I gotta check and see if Lise is coming."

Sophie inhaled sharply, her short gasp echoed through the cold, empty restaurant.

"You okay, Sophie?"

"Did you say Lise?"

"Yeah. Lise. Elise. She said it's been her nickname since she was a kid. As a matter of fact, I think it came from that same uncle I just told you about."

Seventeen
1:00 p.m.

"HE DIDN'T SAY why the kid was here?" Mitch asked.

"No. Only that he was hoping to reconnect with someone."

"What does that mean?"

Elise shook her head slowly and leaned forward in her chair, her fingers sliding down the pen as she turned it over and over on top of Brad's desk. Mitch's frustration over news of the young livery worker was understandable. The kid's odd arrival and limited personal items simply raised more questions for which there were no answers.

"Seems kind of strange someone would just show up in the middle of a storm, looking for work with nothing more than a backpack, don't you think?"

She looked up from the desk in time to see both Brad and Jonathan nod simultaneously to Mitch's rhetorical question. They seemed as interested in the potential lead as she was, yet at just as much of a loss as to what it all meant. Or didn't mean.

"You never saw him?" Jonathan's eyebrows rose upward as he drummed his hands on top of the empty desk where Brad's partner usually sat.

"No. Mr. Stodder said R.J. was sleeping." Elise set the pen down on the desk, scooted her chair backward. "But I have no doubt by the description Mr. Stodder gave us, that this kid he calls R.J. is the same guy Annie mentioned talking to

Thursday night. In fact, I think our sled driver even mentioned him when we were heading to our hotel Thursday afternoon."

Mitch looked upward momentarily before bringing his questioning eyes back to her.

"Don't you remember, Mitch? Joe was surprised there was only one blanket in the sled, but then remembered giving it to a young guy who refused a ride from the airport after the noon flight."

"Yeah, I remember that now. But, if that was the same guy, why did it take from noon until ten o'clock that night for him to try and check into a hotel?"

Elise shrugged. "Good question. And then, when he finally showed up at the livery, he had two blankets, which matches what Annie said. Remember? She felt sorry for him without a winter coat, snuck him an extra one from housekeeping."

She stood and walked over to the front window, watched the blowing snowflakes falling from the sky, snowflakes that seemed to bury everything in their path.

Bury.

The shiver that ran through her body had nothing to do with the swirling flakes or the biting cold that seeped through Brad's partly open window in the far corner of the station. It came from the bone-chilling reality that both Pete and Annie were buried under the snow and her uncle was alone in a remote cabin, shut away from people. A lifestyle that made him a sitting duck for someone looking to hide, someone he didn't even know to fear. Someone who had already struck twice.

"I think one of us needs to head back out to that livery and have a chat with this kid, find out why he's here," Brad said. "I know he's just one of two who tried to check in late that night, but if he's not the one we're looking for, maybe he passed our guy on his way out."

"I agree. But without a working snowmobile and no clue how to ski, I'm kinda useless." Mitch's voice filtered through her ears as she continued to look at the blanket of white that covered everything in her eyesight. "How 'bout you, Jonathan?"

Elise turned from the window and looked at the gray-haired man still sitting behind the empty desk.

"I can't ski either. I suppose I could try, but I might end up being more of a liability than an asset." Jonathan stood up and walked closer to Brad and Mitch. "My father always said I had two left feet when it came to anything athletic."

"I say we call Dan and see if he's interested in heading out to the livery with me." Brad grabbed for the one walkie talkie that was still working.

Mitch reached out, placed a hand on Brad's arm. "I've gotta learn how to ski if I'm gonna be of any use outside this station. So I'll go with you."

Elise's heart sank, her stomach lurched. Mitch's inability to ski had kept him out of harm's way so far. If he learned how to ski well—and she knew in her heart he would—he'd be taking more risks. Risks that might lead him straight into the path of a killer.

"Do you really think this is the time to try?" Her voice, quiet and shaky, brought a hush to the room. "What happens if this kid is the killer? You might need to get away fast."

Mitch's warm brown eyes bore into hers as he spoke. "I'll be fine, Elise. You have to trust in that the way I trusted in you when you insisted on going with the ski group this morning."

He was right. How could she question anything Mitch did when she was holding such a huge part of her life to herself?

"Do you guys want me to hold down the fort here, or head back to the Lakeside Inn to keep an eye on our other suspect?" Jonathan asked.

Mitch grabbed his parka from the coat rack beside the door and handed Jonathan's to him. "Why don't you head over to the hotel now. If you get an opportunity to come back this way in about three hours, then do it. But if Mark's anywhere around, don't."

"Sounds good." Jonathan pulled his parka on and zipped it to his throat. "It seems every pair of pants I own are soaking wet from this snow. Hell, it seems if the killer doesn't get you, the pneumonia will."

He pulled the door open quickly and stepped out into the snow. Elise shivered as she watched the man bend forward against the wind, a single dash of color in a world of pristine white.

"I just wish we had a little more information from the FBI, something to pinpoint an age or a physical characteristic," Elise said quietly.

"That sure would make life easier, wouldn't it?" Brad reached for his gun and slipped it into his shoulder harness. "I feel like we're looking for a needle in a haystack."

"But maybe we don't have to be."

Mitch stopped fiddling with his gloves long enough to stare at her. "What do you mean by that?"

She didn't know why it hadn't occurred to her sooner. It made perfect sense. She turned to Brad, the excitement in her voice a giveaway of the first hopeful feeling she'd had in days. "Does the island paper subscribe to a wire service?"

"A wire service?"

"Like the Associated Press. You know…where they get the news from other parts of the country—places other than here on the island."

"Well, yeah, I guess we do. That's how I read about the case Mitch was working on last summer. Why?"

She clapped her hands together, then reached for her purse. "If the paper subscribes to a wire service then we just might be able to learn something about this killer after all." Her voice rose in pitch as the possibility of finding some much-needed information hit her full force. "Agent Walker said they'd been tracking him for a while and that he's killed others. There's got to be stories about those killings."

"Elise, that's awesome." Mitch ran his hand across his eyes, then over his hair. The excitement in his voice was hard to miss as he turned and looked at his buddy. "Where's the paper's office, Brad?"

"When you get to the bottom of the alleyway out here, you head in the opposite direction of Sophie's. It's the pale blue building on the left-hand side. Merlin Webber's been running that paper for something like twenty years. He knows everything about everything. But fair warning—he's a pretty cranky dude."

"How would we find this guy?" Mitch asked.

"That's easy. He lives above the office."

Elise reached for her coat and scarf, a smile stretching her face for the first time in days. "I know where I'm gonna be while you two are visiting the livery."

MERLIN WEBBER WAS a man who had undoubtedly devoted his entire life to news. She could see it in every corner of the small dusty newsroom, every ceiling-high pile of yellowing paper, every bulletin board covered with multiple layers of highlighted articles, every burned candle that had provided writing time despite the lengthy power failure they faced. And she could almost sense it in the way he studied her, a probing examination that made her feel as if he could see straight through to her soul.

"I'm sorry to bother you, Mr. Webber, but it really is important." Elise extended her hand toward the man, watched the way his thick brows furrowed momentarily then rose as a slow smile crept across his face.

"You say you're a reporter, eh?"

"Yes, I am. For a week—"

Merlin Webber leaned forward, tilted his shiny head in her direction and tapped his ear. "You gotta speak up, honey, I have a slight hearing problem."

Elise smiled and raised her voice an octave. "I work for a weekly paper in Ocean Point, New Jersey."

"Ocean Point, New Jersey, you say?"

And Merlin Webber, the newsman, apparently didn't forget a thing. It was obvious from the moment she said the words that he had connected the name of her town with the events of last summer. She nodded.

"You say your name's Elise Jenkins?"

"Yes."

The man reached his hand out and gripped hers tightly. "I'll say you're a reporter. One helluva reporter."

Embarrassed by the praise, she said, "I take it you heard about the fortuneteller murders?"

"Um, heard about 'em? No honey, I followed that story from the moment the wire services first got hold of it." Merlin turned and led the way toward a desk covered with books and papers, stopping momentarily to push a carelessly stacked mountain of paper off a nearby chair. "Sit. Sit."

Elise unzipped her coat and draped it over the back of the chair, then perched gently on the edge of the seat so as not to wrinkle the few remaining papers left behind. A faint medicinal odor permeated the room, reminded her of the chest rub she'd had to inhale every time she had a childhood cold.

"That final article you wrote—when it was all over— was a mighty fine piece. I'm surprised you didn't get offers from some of the big-time papers to come work for them."

"I did. I just didn't take them up on it. I love my boss too much. He teaches me more about the craft of writing than I ever learned in college. I couldn't walk away from that."

A curious look flashed across the man's face, a look she'd almost bet was grudging respect.

"So what brings you to this island?"

"A vacation. Only it's not what I was envisioning."

"Yeah, this blizzard is a doozy, ain't it?"

If you only knew.

She shifted in her seat, reveled in the warmth that emanated from the kerosene heater in the middle of the room. "Mr. Webber, I don't want to take too much of your ti—"

"Call me Merlin. And there's no need to rush off, I don't have plans. In fact, this is the first time I've been out of bed in over a week thanks to a touch of the flu. I'm a good bit better now, but can't shake this feeling that the world's passed me by while I've been shivering under the covers these past few days."

She studied the man's clean shaven head and face, her gaze coming to rest on the stubby tooth-marked pencil that seemed at home—though a bit cliché—above his right ear. A pencil that would be moving at warp speed if Merlin Webber knew about the murders.

"You don't know, do you?"

The man's piercing gray eyes rounded, his dark eyebrows arched. "Know what?"

Elise took a deep breath and spoke slowly, the disbelief in her voice still evident despite the time she'd had to grasp the events as reality. "There have been two murders here in the last forty-eight hours."

Merlin swiped his hand across his mouth and closed his eyes.

"Mr. Webber, are you okay?"

The man's eyes opened, stared at her from behind thick glasses. "Did you say *two*?"

"I'm afraid so. The first victim was Pete Garner, a skier who was here to participate in an orienteering competition. The second was a young woman who worked as a clerk at the Lakeside Inn."

The legs of the man's chair dropped to the floor. "It wasn't Annie, was it?"

It hadn't occurred to her to consider whether Merlin Webber would know Annie. But of course he would. He was the eyes and ears of Mackinac Island.

Elise reached for the man's hand and squeezed it gently, his skin dry and puffy against hers. "I'm so sorry, Mr. Webber, it didn't even dawn on me that these were people you would know."

Merlin shot his hand upward and shook his head. "No. Don't apologize. What's happened has happened." He reached for a pad of yellow paper and pulled the pencil from his ear. "What do we know at this point?"

She studied the man for a moment, marveled at the way he was able to push his personal feelings aside and focus on the task at hand.

"If you remember my name from the news articles last year then I'm sure you remember the name of my boyfriend—Detective Mitch Burns." She saw the man nod, his head bent close so as not to miss a word she said. "We arrived on the island Thursday afternoon and discovered that Mitch knows one of the police officers here. So we headed over to the station after dinner to spend some time with Brad."

She closed her eyes and tried to recall the fun they'd had walking through the snow after leaving Sophie's that first night. It seemed like a lifetime ago.

"While we were there, Brad got a call from an FBI agent. The agent believed there was a good chance a suspected serial killer had gotten onto the island before the storm started. He wanted Brad to be prepared since the weather was making it impossible for the FBI to get here."

"What do we know about this guy?"

Elise sighed, her shoulders sagged. "Nothing."

Merlin's eyebrows arched once again. "What do you mean *nothing*?"

"Nothing. A sketch of the killer was being faxed over when the power and phone cut out."

Merlin jotted things down on his pad of paper, a string of whispered noises escaping his mouth as he wrote.

Elise continued. "The only thing the agent was able to tell us is that he sometimes takes on the vocation of his last victim."

Merlin's pencil paused in mid air. "I take it we don't know anything about the last victim either?"

"No."

"Any leads so far?"

"We had such hope the agent was wrong. Hope that lasted for just a few short minutes until the captain of the orienteering club walked in to report the disappearance of one of their members. The moment the words were out of his mouth, we suspected the killer was here. Mitch and Brad organized a search party at daybreak and that's when they found the body of the missing skier."

"Maybe he just plain froze out in this weather."

Elise sighed and twisted her gloves with her hands. "He'd been stabbed. Repeatedly."

A low shrill whistle escaped Merlin's lips as he straightened in his chair, a look of naked disbelief momentarily replacing his unreadable features. "Are you serious?"

She frowned down at her hands for a moment before meeting his gaze once again. "Almost from the get-go a man who joined the orienteering competition that morning emerged as a suspect in Mitch's eyes. He's aloof, quiet, even a little surly at times."

"What do *you* think?" Merlin asked as he stood and walked toward the window.

Elise closed her eyes and willed herself to think clearly. "I don't think it's Mark. I talked to him for a long time the night we found Annie. I think he's just a misunderstood loner."

Merlin turned, his eyes hooded and distant below his thick brown eyebrows. "Then go with your gut for now." He crossed the room once again and perched on the edge of his desk. "So what brought you here? To see me?"

She inhaled deeply and squared her shoulders, her spirit buoyed by the opportunity to voice her gut instinct to someone.

"I had a few questions I wanted to ask. Though you've already answered the first one."

Merlin tucked his pencil behind his ear once again. "Oh? What question was that?"

"I was wondering whether you subscribed to a wire service."

The man's head bobbed as he rubbed the raw skin on his face. "I can't imagine not keeping up with the news. It's a window to the troubled soul of our world. Stars are born because of the media. Lives destroyed because of them as well." Merlin's voice trailed off momentarily, then resumed its clarity. "Some people like to pretend the world stops at their door, but it doesn't. And there's no use sticking our heads in the sand pretending that it does."

She noticed the piles of paper that seemed to cover every surface in the room. "Do you keep the stuff you get across the wire?"

"Of course I do. Why?"

She smiled as understanding replaced curiosity in Merlin's eyes.

"Wait! Don't answer that. You're thinking we might find something in an old wire story or two that will give us something to go on."

"You got it. I mean, maybe they don't know *who* this guy is, but knowing something about his crimes might help paint a picture. And at this point anything is better than the nothing we have right now." Elise looked up at the ceiling and closed her eyes momentarily. "In a perfect world, the sketch we didn't receive from the F.B.I. will be on the wire stuff somewhere."

Merlin popped his glasses into his shirt pocket and pushed off the desk. "The service is down now with the power situation and all."

Elise stood and followed Merlin to the small windowless corner on the far side of the newsroom. "Of course it is. I just thought maybe we could wade through any of the stories you already have on file."

Merlin squatted in front of a small cabinet beneath the fax machine. "I keep some of those stories right here."

He pulled a small wooden door open and jumped backward as a pile of papers fell out onto the floor, scattering in different directions.

"I'm so sorry, let me get that." Elise quickly bent down and scooped up a handful of papers, glanced down at the top one on the misshapen pile. "It's hard to be sure in this light, but these look like faxes, not wire stories."

"What?" Merlin looked at the papers in her hand and sighed. "I hired a young high school kid to help me get my files together so I'd have some sort of system for the first time in my life. It doesn't look like her system was any better than mine."

Merlin dropped into a nearby chair and rubbed his eyes. "This low light is really taking a toll on me today. My eyes actually hurt." His voice dropped to a whisper as he continued. "And when I think of Annie, my head hurts, too. She was a real fighter."

Elise stuffed the papers back into the cabinet and shut the door quickly. "I'm so sorry I had to hit you with all of this."

The limited natural light in the room had all but faded as the darkness of an early winter night loomed. "I have an idea. How 'bout I come back in the morning when we have more light. We can go through the past six to twelve months of wire stories and see what we come up with. And until then, you can try to get some rest. You don't look as if you've completely licked that flu."

Merlin swiped his hand across his eyes again. "I never imagined stuff like this could happen here. And now that it has, I'm laid up, dealing with the remnants of some damn bug. Figures, doesn't it?"

"Don't worry about it. We'll put our heads together in the morning."

Merlin walked her toward the door, his hands jammed into the pockets of his jeans. "Just come on in when you get here. Maybe a good night's sleep will help, though I doubt I'll be able to resist the urge to find what I can before bed."

Elise pulled her coat from the chair as she walked by, slipped her arms into the sleeves and pulled the zipper to her chin.

"Okay, but no worries if you don't," she said, tugging her gloves onto her hands. "I better head out. Mitch and Brad should be back from the livery by now."

"Good. You don't need to be on your own in that station. You've got good instincts, I can tell. But all the same, don't let your guard down around this Mark guy you told me about. Just in case Mitch is right. Someone had to have killed that skier."

"And Annie."

Merlin inhaled slowly, his shoulders sagged. "And Annie."

She reached out and squeezed his hand one last time. "I'll see you in the morning. Good night, Mr. Webber. Try to get some rest."

"Merlin. Call me Merlin."

Eighteen
5:30 p.m.

ELISE COULD SENSE the tension the second she opened the door. It hung in the air like a thick heavy storm cloud.

"I was just getting ready to head down to the paper to check on you." Mitch covered the distance between Brad's desk and the door in seconds, pulled her in for a hug. "I missed you."

"I missed you, too."

"Um, guys? Do you want me to leave?"

Elise looked over Mitch's shoulder at Brad, his boyish grin a contrast to the worry in his eyes. There was no doubt about it. Something was up.

She kissed Mitch's mouth gently, then pulled back to look into his golden brown eyes. "What happened? Did you meet R.J.?"

Mitch ran his hand across his eyes and through his hair, exhaled slowly through puffed cheeks.

"We never made it to the livery."

Elise looked from Mitch to Brad and back again. "Why not? Did you have trouble with the skiing?"

"No. Mitch took to skiing like he does everything else." Brad pulled his desk chair out, sat down, and leaned back against the wall. "He was actually faster than me on the way back here."

Elise waited for something that would explain the tension in Mitch's body, the worry in Brad's eyes.

"We decided to check out the rental place on the way out to the livery. To see who rented skis Thursday morning."

"And?"

"No one did. But the killer's been there. Just as he's been here."

She stared at Mitch for a long moment, her mind reeling with a million questions at once.

"Here?"

Mitch nodded, his eyes fixed on hers. "Brad and the hotel clerk, Tom, didn't just run out of gas in their snowmobiles. It was drained."

"Drained? How do you know that?"

"Because every one of the fifteen snowmobiles in the rental shop barn were empty despite having been filled up Thursday morning. And they haven't been used since then."

She gasped. The killer was circling, waiting.

Mitch's warm arms pulled her close once again, his lips pressed against her forehead, her temple. "It's okay, Lise. We're gonna be okay."

She waited for his words to stop the familiar fear in her heart, but they didn't. This guy, whoever he was, was toying with them. Simply because he could.

Pulling her lower lip inward, Elise willed herself to find strength in Mitch's arms. She had to. It was the only thing she could draw on right now. That and the possibility that she might find something at Merlin's that could give them the upper hand.

When she finally spoke, her voice was soft yet determined. "We can't let this guy beat us."

She felt Mitch's warm breath against her ear. "That's my girl."

"Hey, how'd it go with Webber?" Brad asked.

Elise pulled away from Mitch and leaned against the half wall that separated the tiny waiting area from the rest of the station.

"It went well. I filled him in on what we're dealing with and asked him about the wire service." Elise unzipped her coat and slipped her arms out. "He's got one and has actually kept all of the stories from the past year."

Mitch whistled. "That's gotta be a lot of stories."

Elise nodded. "It is. Which is one reason why the place is almost wall to wall paper."

"Did you find anything?"

She shook her head, drummed her fingers along the edge of the wall. "By the time I finished filling him in on everything, the lighting inside the newsroom was simply too poor to see anything. And Merlin was moving slow."

Brad's laugh echoed against the bare white cinderblock walls. "Merlin? Slow? That geezer might be a lot of things but slow ain't one of 'em."

"He's recovering from the flu. He's had it so bad that he didn't have an inkling about what's been going on around here the past few days."

"I was wonderin' where he's been. That man doesn't miss anything." Brad set the front legs of his chair back down on the ground and stood.

Elise followed Brad across the room with her eyes, watched him push the rear window up a few inches.

"It's a wonder we're all not sick with your bizarre need for fresh air." Mitch shook his head with mock irritation then leaned on the wall beside Elise.

"It's part of my charm, remember?" Brad quipped.

"The chicks dig it." Elise laughed as the words left her mouth, her impression of Brad almost flawless.

Mitch laughed out loud, a joyous sound that Elise realized she'd missed more than anything else these past few days. She desperately wanted the relaxed Mitch who had sat beside her on the sleigh ride to the hotel. The Mitch who deserved a break.

"That was perfect, Elise."

She curtseyed to the floor, savored the momentary pause in their cruel reality. "Thank you, kind sir."

"Okay, okay, smart alecks." Brad slid the window down a quarter of an inch and headed back toward his desk chair. "So I guess we'll need to check in with Merlin tomorrow to see if he's found anything?"

"No, you guys have enough on your plate without having to look through endless paper piles. This is something I can do."

"What are you thinking you're gonna find?" Brad reached into his top desk drawer and pulled out a box of green Tic Tacs. "Want one?"

Elise put her hand up quickly, shook her head. "What I'm hoping to find is a story—or series of stories—about the crimes this guy has committed. If we do, that could really fill in some much-needed pieces for us."

"Man, that would be awesome." Brad popped a mint into his mouth and leaned forward on his desk, swinging his gaze from Elise, to Mitch, and back again. "But how do you even know where to start?"

"Agent Walker said they were tracking the killer across several states. That this guy assumes the vocation of his victims, right? That's the kind of story that papers pick up. It might be a small story out of Bu-Fu, Iowa, but something like that will get picked up by the wires eventually." Elise leaned against Mitch, savored the feel of his arm across her shoulders, his breath against her head. "But I'll be honest, I'm hoping for even more than that."

"What's that?"

She turned her head and looked at Mitch, saw the curiosity in his eyes as he waited for her to answer.

"A picture."

8:45 p.m.

She leaned against the door and closed her eyes. As much as she wanted to cuddle in Mitch's arms all night, she simply needed some time alone. To think, plan.

And Mitch needed the sleep. His eyes looked sunken, his cheeks flushed. The last thing they needed was for him to get sick and he knew that as well as she did.

Elise turned her ear to the door and listened, heard the muffled sound of footsteps followed by silence. Mitch was in bed, where he belonged.

She looked slowly around her room, shined the small flashlight at the flowered walls, the thick drapes, the old fashioned dressing mirror, the elegant comforter, and her purse.

She pushed off the door and sat down on the edge of the bed, pulled the small leather bag off the antique nightstand and reached inside. The photograph was worn in the middle, the colors muted with time. But the smile on her uncle's face was as bright and full of life as it was in her memories, a cruel contrast to the man he had apparently become.

Closing her eyes, she thought back to the day everything changed. The day her aunt had been found dead and everyone turned against her uncle.

Even now, thirteen years later, she still didn't believe Uncle Ken had been negligent. It wasn't in his nature to be careless. And he had absolutely adored Faye.

Elise swiped at the tear that ran down her cheek.

The pieces of that day had never fit together for Elise like they had for the rest of the family. It just seemed impossible to her that Uncle Ken would have forgotten to go back into the garage to shut off his hotrod before he left for work. But even if he *had* forgotten, it was a tragic accident. An accident he had to live with for the rest of his life, one that cost him his wife. And little Ray.

She looked at the picture in her hand again, at Uncle Ken's face-splitting smile, Aunt Faye's gentle beauty, little Ray's sparkling ocean-blue eyes. Faye had always referred to the day she met Uncle Ken as a miracle. The kind of day that made you believe in dreams.

"Elise, I never thought I'd find happiness after Raymond died, never thought little Ray could have another dad who loved him like Raymond did. But your uncle proved me wrong."

Their wedding had been like something out of a storybook. Elise had been the flower girl, little Ray the ring bearer. And the love the three of them had for one another was as tangible as the flowers Elise had carried.

Fortunately for her, Faye had accepted Elise's frequent visits with open arms. She'd seemed to understand that Elise saw their happy home as a breath of fresh air. They'd included her in picnics and outings, camping trips and holidays, and even occasional vacations like their trip to Mackinac.

The island vacation had been perfect, the sun shining down on them the entire week. There had been bike rides and hikes, picnics and walks. And they'd all giggled at the image of a gray-haired Uncle Ken and toothless Aunt Faye sitting on the porch of the log home they'd fallen in love with during one of their walks.

A log home that Uncle Ken had fled to in grief. Alone.

Elise stood, walked to the window that overlooked Lake Huron. The brief respite between storms was over; blowing snow was falling on the remote island once again.

She glanced down at the picture in her hand, at the image that was barely visible in the darkened room. Uncle Ken was alone in that cabin. Shut away from a world that had turned against him at a time when he desperately needed love and understanding.

And now he was a sitting duck, a perfect target for a madman looking to hide in a place where no one ever went.

Turning, Elise picked up the flashlight and shone it on the roll top desk in the corner of her room. She walked to the chair and sat, reached for the hotel's pen and paper and began to write.

Uncle Ken might not answer a knock at the door, but she was hopeful he'd answer if he knew true understanding was on the other side.

Sunday, January 30th
Nineteen
7:00 a.m.

ELISE PULLED THE soft green turtleneck over her head and stared at her image in the mirror. The constant tossing and turning throughout the night showed in the dull eyes that stared back, lifeless, guilty.

How on earth was she going to get to the cabin and back without Mitch knowing? Could she slip away when he thought she was with Merlin?

Just the notion of being dishonest with Mitch made her cheeks redden, her shoulders slump. But she didn't know what else to do.

Elise stuck her tongue out at herself and turned around, her gaze suddenly riveted on a small square of paper sliding toward her feet.

She squatted down, stared at the familiar writing.

Elise,

> *I'm heading over to the station early to toss some things around with Brad. No need to rush over. I'm hoping you'll sleep in and take some time for you.*
> *I Love You!*

Mitch

She stared at the note, her heart racing. If she hurried, she could get out to the cabin and back before Mitch even knew she was awake!

Elise heard the click of Mitch's outer door followed by the sound of his footsteps as he headed toward the stairs at the end of the hall.

She stood and walked to the window that overlooked the front entrance and peered down. Moments later, Mitch emerged from the building, his legs sinking into the deep snow as he headed in the direction of the station.

It's now or never, Elise.

She grabbed her coat from the rack in the corner, stepped into her tall black boots. Even after nearly twelve hours, they still felt cold and wet. If she never saw another snowflake again it would be too soon.

But at least she had her skis. It was the one thing that would make the trek across the island even close to doable.

8:10 a.m.

Elise could hear the pounding of her heart beneath her ear muffs, feel her hands moisten inside her gloves as she rounded the last cropping of trees that separated her from the cabin.

The light colored logs that had caught Aunt Faye's attention nearly fourteen years ago had darkened—a casualty of age and years of harsh winter weather. The windows that had once seemed so full of character and light were now covered with dark fabric to keep the world out. The front porch was void of the Adirondack chairs Uncle Ken had dreamed of and the hanging flowers Faye had described in great detail.

In fact, if it wasn't for the plumes of smoke that rose from the chimney, there would be no indication of life inside at all.

Elise stopped, her breath coming in short tired gasps. Now that she was here, she was scared. Scared that he wouldn't open the door. Scared that he'd turn her away.

But she had to try.

Squaring her shoulders, Elise dug her poles into the ground and pushed off, the fear in her heart giving way to tempered anticipation.

With several quick strides she reached the base of the front porch, bent down and released her boots from the skis. Her legs felt like rubber as she stepped onto the weathered porch and walked toward the door, her hands sweating inside her gloves.

"Knock, Elise." The whispered words escaped her dry mouth, disappeared in the cold winter air.

Trembling, she raised her hand and knocked, softly at first, then with more urgency as her efforts went unanswered.

Finally she stopped, pulled off her gloves, and reached into the pocket of her coat. The slip of paper was there, waiting.

Elise unfolded the white square and stared at the tear-stained words she'd written by flashlight. Words she prayed would make the difference.

She bent down and gently maneuvered the paper through the miniscule crack beneath the door, then knocked one last time.

Seconds turned to minutes as she waited, her ears straining to make out any sign of life on the other side of the door.

But there was nothing.

"Please, Uncle Ken, please open the door."

Her voice rose as she knocked harder.

"I have to talk to you. I *need* to talk to you."

Cold, salty tears ran into her mouth as she knocked again and again, her head pleading with her heart to stop. He wasn't going to answer. He had shut her out, too.

Crying, she turned from the door and headed back to her skis, her legs stiff and heavy. It was no use. He wanted nothing to do with anyone. Including her.

A soft click made her turn. The door slowly opened, revealing the tall, bearded man she hadn't seen in years.

Strong arms reached for her as she crumbled to the ground, sobbing.

"It's okay, Elise. I'm here."

8:10 a.m.

Mitch looked at the sheet of paper in front of him, moved his finger slowly down the list he'd just completed.

"All we've got is Mark and that's too easy."

"Huh?"

Mitch looked up from his list and stared at Brad. "C'mon Brad, you need to wake up."

"I'm trying, man. That damn kerosene heater is making me tired." Brad pushed his chair back and stood, walked toward the window. "If you want me to be alert you're gonna have to put up with the window being open."

"Whatever works. I just need you following me." Mitch gulped the black coffee Sophie had given him as he passed by her restaurant that morning. "It's gonna be a while 'til the Feds get out here with this much snow and more waves coming all the time. We've gotta get more proactive."

Brad unlatched the window and pushed it upward. "We're doing what we can. And since Annie, there's been nothing else."

"That we know of." Mitch ran his hand across his eyes and over his hair. "Hell, there could be dead bodies sitting in some of those outlying homes you've got on your map and we wouldn't have a clue."

"There's a nice thought." Brad puffed up his cheeks. "What were you saying before about Mark not fitting?"

Mitch looked back down at the list he'd written. "If there's one thing I've learned over the past year, it's that the obvious is rarely your answer. Agent Walker said this guy would be under our nose but he didn't say he was stupid. And Mark was very forthcoming with Elise when she interviewed him."

"Okay, so now what?"

As much as Mitch enjoyed his friendship with Brad, it was hard not to get frustrated with the guy. He simply didn't like anything that was hard. Which was probably why he'd secured a job in a place where nothing ever happened.

Until now.

"So now we start talking to all the residents, get details about every new face they've seen since Thursday."

"Yeah, but most everyone is holed up in their homes or hotel rooms. How much help is that gonna be?"

Mitch's gaze moved across the desk, lingered on the coffee cup. "Their vocations."

"Huh?"

"Vocations." Mitch straightened in his chair. "Agent Walker said this guy takes on the vocation of his victims. What did Pete do for a living?"

"I think one of those guys said he was a computer guy of some sort. But I don't think anyone's parading around pretending to be a computer geek, do you?"

Brad was right. It didn't make sense.

"Wait, Mitch, here comes Jonathan."

Mitch looked toward the front windows and saw Jonathan shaking snow from his trousers and coat on the front porch.

He pushed his chair back and stood, walked quickly toward the front door just as the tall, grey-haired man entered the station.

"Good morning, boys."

Mitch reached for Jonathan's leather-clad hand. "Hey, Jonathan. We're glad you're here. How'd it go last night?"

Jonathan pulled his gloves off and stuck them in his pocket, unbuttoned his coat slowly. "I made a point of sitting down in the lobby by the fireplace hoping I could strike up a conversation with anyone else who happened to be down there."

Mitch hung Jonathan's coat on the rack beside his own.

"Anything interesting?"

"Maybe. Mark came downstairs at one point and seemed kinda edgy. Asked if I thought you were at the station."

"Really?"

"Yeah. At first I was a little nervous that he'd put it together and figured out I was a cop too, but I don't think he did."

"Did he say why he was asking about me?"

Jonathan shook his head. "Nope. Just said he had something he needed to run by you. I didn't want to prod too much for fear that'd raise his suspicion."

Mitch nodded, his thoughts reeling. "Do you have any idea what it might have been about?"

Jonathan shrugged. "No. He wasn't interested in telling me anything."

"Maybe we should head up there now and find out what his deal is." Brad reached for his coat and pulled it from the rack.

Jonathan raised his hand. "Hold on there a minute, Brad. You can't do that."

"Why not?"

Mitch spoke, his voice quiet yet firm as he enunciated each word in an attempt to help Brad understand. "Because then Mark will know that Jonathan is reporting back to us."

"Oh. You're right."

Mitch rubbed his eyes, willed himself not to say something he was going to regret. But it was obvious by Jonathan's rigid stance that Mitch was not the only one who was growing irritated with Brad's cluelessness.

"I say we just hang here for a little while and see if he shows up," Mitch said.

"I think that's a good idea. I'm gonna head over to Sophie's for some coffee and then check back later." Jonathan reached for his coat then stopped, looked around. "Where's Elise?"

Mitch looked down at his wrist as he spoke. "At the hotel. Hopefully getting some much-needed sleep. But she should be here soon."

8:50 a.m.

ELISE PULLED THE afghan closer, watched as a log broke in two—sending sparks up the chimney.

"Are you warm enough?"

She pulled her gaze from the glowing embers in the hearth, focused on Uncle Ken's concerned face.

"I'm fine. I'm just so glad to see you—I've missed you so much."

Uncle Ken cleared his throat, brushed a hand across his mouth. "I've missed you too, Lise."

Now that she was here, with him, the years that had come and gone since she had last seen him disappeared like the tiny sparks that shot out from the fire and vanished into thin air. Sure, the beard was new and his eyes no longer held their enchanting sparkle. But he was here. Safe.

She pulled the afghan tighter and peered around the cabin. There wasn't much furniture, just the essentials. But what was there provided a cozy feel.

"Where did you get all of this stuff?" She asked softly.

"I bought it with the cabin. There're only a few things that are mine."

She followed his gaze to a row of pictures that adorned the half wall separating the kitchen and sitting room. Aunt Faye smiled from one of the frames, little Ray from another.

Uncle Ken cleared his throat again, reached for her hand. "What brings you here? To Mackinac?"

"I told myself that I came just to get away from work and enjoy some time with my boyfriend, Mitch." She looked down at Uncle Ken's hand on hers. "But I guess I really wanted to come here to connect with a place that held a lot of happiness for me."

She felt his hand squeeze hers and she looked up, met his sad eyes with her own.

"I'm sorry, Lise. I just needed to leave, distance myself from everyone. The hatred they all have for me is nothing compared to the hatred I have for myself."

Elise slid off the chair, sunk to her knees in front of Uncle Ken's chair. "*I* don't hate you. I know you didn't set out to hurt Aunt Faye. I know how much you loved her. I can't explain why they all turned on you like that. But *I* didn't. I know it was an accident. I've never doubted that for a minute."

She looked up at Uncle Ken, saw the tear that slid from beneath his closed eyelids. Pushing herself off the ground, Elise wrapped her arms around the once muscular body and waited for the trembling to stop.

"I love you, Uncle Ken," she whispered.

THE ATMOSPHERE IN the cabin felt different. Almost as if there was a tiny glimmer of hope.

She pushed off the couch and walked around the room, her eyes drawn to the breathtaking photographs that hung on the walls.

"You're still taking pictures?"

"On occasion. From my porch."

"I always thought you were the best photographer around. I loved watching the pictures appear on the paper in the darkroom. It was always so magical."

"Yeah, well, I enjoyed it, too. You were always so eager to ask questions, listen to the answers. You seemed to really want to learn about the darkroom."

"I did. I do. Is there one here?"

"Of course."

She wandered back to the couch and sat, peered at Uncle Ken as he moved around the small kitchen area, opening cans and rustling in drawers.

"There's not much I can offer to feed you with no power, but some of these canned provisions are actually pretty okay."

His words filtered through the air, settled in her thoughts. She'd never really stopped to think how he survived in isolation. Until now.

"How do you get your food? Do you go into town?"

"I haven't stepped foot off my property since the day I got here."

"Then how, how do you—"

"My afternoon angel."

"Your what?"

"My afternoon angel. The only thing that's kept me going all these years." Uncle Ken strode into the room carrying a tray with two plates. "But that's enough about me. I want to catch up on you."

He set the tray on top of the floor. "I hope you like beef stew for breakfast. Shouldn't take too long to warm it up on the fire."

"Beef stew sounds wonderful." She scooted the rocking chair closer to the hearth, watched as her uncle placed a small pot onto a cooking surface just above the logs. "Sitting here, with you, I've almost forgotten about the serial killer."

Uncle Ken turned from the fire. "Serial killer?"

Elise nodded slowly, filled her uncle in on everything that had happened since her arrival on the island. She watched his face harden as he listened, saw his jaw tighten.

"I saw someone cutting through my property Thursday morning, seemed to be real aware of his surroundings."

She stared at Uncle Ken's face, waited for him to continue.

"When you're in one spot for as long as I've been, you develop a sort of intuition about things around you and I sensed something was off that morning. I pulled back that curtain just enough to see this kid standing there, staring at the cabin."

Elise leaned forward. "What do you remember about him?"

Uncle Ken twisted the end of his beard between his fingers. "He was young. Looked like he had on a blue coat or cape of some sort. Had two white things in his hand. But then

I think he spotted me at the window, cuz the next thing I knew he was in a sprint through the woods."

"Could you see anything else?"

"He dropped one of the white things when he took off."

Elise jumped to her feet. "Maybe I can find it."

"No. Not in all the snow we've had since then."

She walked toward the window Uncle Ken had indicated and peeked outside. Sure enough, the snow was piled high beside the shed, too deep to wade through.

"Did he have red hair?" Elise turned from the window, met Uncle Ken's curious eyes.

"Nah. Brown. Maybe a little wavy."

"Brown?"

Annie's voice suddenly filled her thoughts.

"Besides, he was kinda cute, ya know? Had a thick head of gorgeous wavy brown hair, and blue eyes that just took your breath away..."

"Yup. Brown. Why?"

"Mitch has been focusing on a redhead but my gut says he's wrong. Maybe I'm right after all."

"Maybe." Uncle Ken pulled the pot from the fire and ladled the stew onto their plates. "This boyfriend of yours—Mitch. Is he good to you?"

Elise walked back to the hearth and reached for the plate Uncle Ken held out. "He's wonderful. He's *my* angel."

"I'm glad."

They ate in silence, a feeling of warmth now blanketing a room that felt so cold only an hour ago. She prayed that Uncle Ken felt the difference, too.

A succession of low beeps broke through the quiet of the cabin, made her jump.

"It's just my watch, Lise. It must be ten-thirty."

"Ten-thirty? Oh my God, I have to go! Mitch is gonna be worried if I'm not at the station soon." She set the plate down on the tray and reached for Uncle Ken's hands. "Please come with me. Come to the station and tell Mitch about the guy on your property."

"I can't do that, Lise."

She stared at him, saw the dull film that inched across his eyes. "Why not?"

"I just can't."

Her heart ached for the man who stood in front of her, the man who died a different death the moment Faye was found.

"Then let me bring Mitch here. You're too vulnerable out here by yourself."

"No."

Reaching upward, she cupped his bristly cheek in her palm. "Okay. But I'll be back soon. Alone."

Twenty
11:45 a.m.

SHE COULD SEE Mitch pacing around the station room, his shoulders rigid, his jaw tightened. Brad was in his usual chair, leaning against the wall with his arms behind his head, completely oblivious to the effects his open window had on the core temperature of everyone else in the room. Jonathan seemed tired, wary, his eyes tracking Mitch back and forth across the floor.

Elise inhaled slowly, the cold snowy air searing her lungs. She was going to have some serious explaining to do, that was for sure. But the true reason for her extended "sleep" would have to wait. It would be hard enough to tell Mitch about Uncle Ken alone, she certainly didn't need to divulge her long-held secret in front of an audience.

She turned the doorknob and pushed, snow falling from her sleeve with the quick movement of her arm.

"Elise! Oh my God, where've you been?"

The worry in Mitch's eyes was unmistakable as he crossed the room to meet her, his forehead creased with concern.

"I was, um, resting—like you said." She felt Mitch's powerful arms around her shoulders, his strong hand on the back of her head, and the overwhelming guilt in her heart at the lies that continued to pour from her mouth. "Did I miss something?"

Mitch's warm lips pressed against her forehead, her eyes, before he finally stepped back.

"It's almost noon, Lise! I was a few seconds away from sending out a search party to check the hotel."

"It's true, Elise. He's been pacing so hard I thought he was gonna wear a hole right through the middle of the floor." Brad stood and walked around his desk to stand beside Jonathan. "It took all my powers of persuasion to keep him from breaking down your door and interrupting your beauty sleep."

She pulled her lower lip inward for a moment and looked from Mitch, to Brad, to Jonathan, and back again.

"I'm sorry, guys. I ju—, I just needed some time. For me."

Elise searched Mitch's face, silently prayed for him to understand, to somehow accept her lie as truth. But his eyes showed no indication of mistrust. Only fear. For her.

Nibbling on her lip, she forced her eyes to stay focused on him, to resist the impulse to look down at her feet in shame. Finally, his stance loosened and he pulled her to him once again.

"I'm okay, Mitch, really," she whispered. "I'm sorry I worried you."

After several long moments his grip loosened and she stepped back, her heart still heavy with guilt, her mind searching for something to say to take the focus off of her.

"Did I miss anything this morning?" Elise heard the tremor in her voice, hoped the guys didn't notice.

Jonathan coughed and leaned back against Brad's desk. "Nothing other than the fact that Mark has something he wants to show Mitch."

She looked at Mitch, willed herself to see past the added tension in his face. Tension she had caused.

"What is it?"

Mitch shook his head, ran his hand across his eyes and over his hair. "Don't know. He hasn't come by."

Elise looked back at Jonathan, questions whirling through her thoughts faster than she could comprehend. "He didn't tell you what it was?"

"Nope. And I couldn't ask without looking suspicious."

She looked back at Mitch. "So are you gonna wait here to see if he comes?"

Mitch shook his head once again. "No. Brad and I want to head out to the livery and talk to Vic's kid since we never made it out there yesterday."

Elise pulled the sleeve of her parka back to reveal the silver watch underneath. "Oh my gosh, Merlin! I completely forgot."

"Elise, I don't know if I want you on your own again, I'm not sure I'm ready for that."

The intense honesty in Mitch's voice stung and she silently berated herself for causing him an added strain he didn't need or deserve. She reached out, touched Mitch's arm. "Mitch, I'm okay. I'll be fine."

"I can go with Elise, if that'll help," Jonathan offered. "It'll give me something to do, and there shouldn't be any reason that Mark would see us together in a newsroom."

Elise looked up and met Mitch's questioning eyes with a smile. "See? I'll be fine. Please don't worry about me."

"That's like asking me not to breathe, Elise."

12:45 p.m.

"THAT YOUNG MAN really loves you."

Jonathan's words hung like clouds in the still air as they trudged side by side through the snow.

Elise stopped, looked up at the retired officer's piercing green eyes.

"I love him, too, Jonathan."

"Oh, I have no doubt about that. It's written across your face every bit as much as his." Small puffs of smoke escaped the man's mouth as his warm breath met the cold air. "But I saw something else in your face back at the station just now."

Elise jammed her gloved-hands into the pockets of her parka and continued walking, her heart rate accelerating as Jonathan fell in step beside her once again.

"Look, I'm not trying to pry into something that isn't my business, but you can't be thrown into a situation like the one we're in and not begin to care about the people around you."

"It has nothing to do with whether I love Mitch," she said, her voice quiet, yet uncharacteristically raspy. "It's about me. My family."

"And Mitch doesn't know?"

Elise shook her head, silence filling the space between them as they stepped onto the front porch of the Island News.

"I just, well, it's not something...oh, Jonathan...it's complicated." She looked up at his face, knew her eyes were pleading with him to understand and not judge.

"It's okay, Elise, you don't have to explain anything to me. But if you want to talk, I've been told that I'm a pretty good listener."

"Thanks, Jonathan."

"No problem. Now, let's see if this news guy can help us out a little."

Nodding, she turned and knocked loudly. Several long minutes passed before the door finally opened and Merlin's face peeked out slowly from around the corner.

"Hi Merlin, how're you feeling today?"

The newsman looked her over from head to toe then turned his attention on Jonathan, his eyes sporting an odd look she'd put somewhere between curiosity and annoyance.

"Who's he?"

"This is Jonathan. He's helping Mitch and Brad with their investigation." Elise stepped aside to allow Jonathan to extend his hand to Merlin, a gesture that was met with no response.

"I'm sorry, Merlin, I suppose I should have checked with you to make sure it was okay."

Jonathan kept his hand out, waited for Merlin to reciprocate. "Mr. Webber, it's not Elise's fault that I'm here. I just thought maybe three sets of eyes would be better than two."

She was relieved when Merlin finally gripped Jonathan's hand and pulled the door open completely.

"Sorry. I guess I'm just a bit on edge after everything you told me yesterday, Elise." Merlin shut the door behind them and turned toward the newsroom across the narrow hall.

"So, are you feeling any better, Merlin?"

"A little. I slept pretty hard until about eight o'clock. But then I couldn't stay away from the wire files any longer."

"Did you find anything?" Jonathan's firm, gruff voice boomed through the paper-crammed room as he scanned the office, slowly bringing his eyes back to Elise and Merlin.

"Not a thing." Merlin gestured toward the ground beneath the back left window. "I've already gone through the pile to the left of the basket, but haven't actually gotten to the ones inside it yet."

Elise unbuttoned her coat and pulled her arms out, draped the baby blue parka across a nearby chair. "Okay, then I'll start there."

Merlin addressed Jonathan, his probing tone a reflection of his chosen profession. "Do you have a news background, too?"

Jonathan shook his head, a slight smile turning the corners of his mouth upward. "No. I'm a retired cop."

"A cop?"

"Yup."

"Did you come over here with Elise and her detective friend?"

"No. We just met the other day."

"Then how do we know you're really a cop and not the serial killer masquerading as a cop?"

The silence that blanketed the newsroom was deafening. Elise felt her mouth drop open as she struggled to think of something to help soften Merlin's attitude.

"Good for you for checking on me," Jonathan said as he reached into his back pocket and pulled out a badge. "More people need to ask questions, particularly in a situation like this."

She felt the tension in her shoulders ease as Merlin squinted approvingly at the badge Jonathan placed in his hand.

"Sorry, Jonathan. I had to ask."

Jonathan's hand shot into the air and he shook his head emphatically. "No apologies needed, Mr. Webber."

Merlin coughed into his balled-up fist, then ran his hand across his mouth. "Call me Merlin. Now, I'd offer you some coffee, but that's kinda tough without electricity at the moment. How 'bout a Pepsi? Elise?"

"That'd be great, Merlin. Thanks. How about you, Jonathan?"

"No, nothing for me. I'm fine right now."

Merlin disappeared into the narrow front hallway, leaving Elise and Jonathan alone in the newsroom.

"I'm sorry about Merlin's twenty questions just then."

"Don't be. He's a newsman. He's built to be skeptical." Jonathan unzipped his coat and placed it on top of Elise's. "Now let's get at the rest of those stories in that basket while we still have some natural light to work by."

They sat on the floor side by side, each reaching for a stack of unread papers from the blue plastic basket.

1:45 p.m.

"IT'S RIGHT AROUND that corner." Brad raised his arm and pointed with his ski pole in the direction of Stodder's Livery.

Mitch nodded and pushed against the ground with his pole, anxious to finally meet the stable owner's new employee. There was no doubt, the kid's time of arrival on the island left many questions.

They skied straight for a few hundred yards, then turned just beyond the final cropping of trees. Sure enough, as they rounded the corner, an old wooden barn sprang into view. Plumes of smoke billowed from the chimney of the A-frame cedar house that stood just to the right of the barn.

Mitch skied to a stop beside Brad.

"Let's head straight to the barn and see if we can catch this guy without warning."

Brad looked toward the house. "I dunno, Mitch. Vic Stodder doesn't take too kindly to people being on his property and he ain't shy about using his gun."

"Then you head on up to the house. I'll head over to the barn." Mitch unsnapped his skis and stepped into the snow. "That way you can thwart the whole gun-threatening thing, and I can catch this kid off guard."

Brad unsnapped his skis and headed toward the house, glancing back over his shoulder at Mitch. "Are you sure about this?"

"Yes. Go."

Mitch trudged through the snow to the barn, stopped just outside the partially opened door. He could hear someone talking in a quiet, soothing voice.

He stepped inside. A row of stalls lined the right wall, another row the left. The hushed, soothing words were coming from a stall in the back.

Quietly, Mitch made his way down the center aisle, stopping just before the last stall on the right.

A brown-haired kid in his late teens was kneeling beside a foal, talking softly as he held a bottle to the animal's lips.

Mitch leaned forward, strained to make out the young man's words.

"I know what it's like to lose someone important. But you're gonna be okay cuz I'm here with you. And even though that doesn't bring your mom back, it does help."

Mitch deliberately stepped forward, stamped his snow-covered boots on the packed earth.

The young man jumped up, dropped the bottle, and reached for a pitchfork in the corner of the stall. "Don't come any closer."

Mitch held his arms upward and stood still. "Hold on there. You're okay. My name's Mitch Burns. Detective Mitch Burns."

The young man's shoulders sagged in relief. "You scared me. Vic told me to keep my guard up in this storm. Does he know you're here?"

Mitch shook his head slowly. "I came to ask you a few questions."

"Me?"

"Yeah. I understand you arrived on the island Thursday night?"

"Thursday afternoon, actually."

"Then why didn't you end up here until after ten that night? Isn't that kinda late to be trekking around a strange island looking for a place to stay?"

The young man shrugged, his cheeks reddened. "I suppose. But I chickened out of doing what I came here to do. I tried to make myself put the letter under the door but I got scared."

"Letter?"

The young man kicked softly at the straw in the stall. "Yeah. I've got a letter I need to give someone, a letter that I'm hoping will make a big difference in his life. And in mine, too. But I just couldn't make myself do it. I don't know why. So I walked around the island, in the snow, trying to find some courage. But it didn't work. Then I realized I better find a place to sleep, so I started checking hotels. Asking for work in exchange for a room."

Mitch searched the kid's face, looked for any signs of deception. But there were none.

"The girl behind the counter at the last hotel said they didn't need any help, but was nice enough to point me in Vic's direction. She even gave me an extra blanket to wrap up in 'cuz I wasn't real prepared for how cold it is here."

"What's your name?"

"R.J." He stepped around the small horse and reached a hand in Mitch's direction.

"You look like you know something about animals."

R.J. nodded, looked back at the horse for a moment. "Spent the past thirteen years living on my grandparent's farm. In fact, it's the one good thing that came out of those years.

Little Belle here lost her mamma. I guess this weather and birthing was just too much for her."

Mitch looked at the foal for a moment, digesting everything R.J. had said. As much as he'd hoped to find some much-needed answers about the killer, it was obvious that he wouldn't find them here at the livery.

Unless…

"Do you remember passing anyone when you left that last hotel?"

R.J. skewed his jaw to the side and squinted at the water trough along the wall. "Well, kinda. I did pass one dude who looked really cold. He was just covered in snow. I offered him one of my blankets, but he didn't say anything. Just kept walking."

"What did he look like?"

"Hard to tell. His hood was real close around his face and he was looking down the whole time. There was some hair sticking out, but it was covered in snow like everything else on him."

Mitch nodded, his mind replaying R.J.'s description. "Well, thanks for your time, R.J. I hope you get to deliver that letter soon."

The young man's eyes moistened and he blinked quickly. "I will. I have to. I just need to find the right time."

3:15 p.m.

SHE KNEW THE defeat in Jonathan's eyes was a mirror of her own. A year's worth of wire stories had yielded nothing about their serial killer.

"You would think someone like this would get national attention, but that's not the way it works, is it, Elise? The media prefers to focus on politics, and Hollywood celebrities with their messed-up lives."

Elise looked up and saw Merlin standing above her, his hands jammed into the front pockets of his baggy jeans.

"Oh, I don't agree with that. I just think this guy hasn't struck enough yet to make the wires, that's all."

Merlin snorted and walked to the window, his shoulders rigid with tension as he looked out at the darkening sky.

Elise grimaced at the numbness in her legs as she stood for the first time in two hours. The helplessness of their situation was getting to all of them in different ways. Merlin was growing tenser by the moment. *Her* energy level was rapidly decreasing, a touch of depression no doubt.

She looked at Jonathan as he scoured each remaining piece of paper in his pile.

"I take it you're coming up empty, too?"

Jonathan looked up. "So far. But give me ten minutes, Elise, I've got a few more stories to get through." Jonathan's voice trailed off as his eyes, once again, returned to the papers in his hand.

Elise shrugged and walked around the room, grateful for the opportunity to stretch her legs. She couldn't help but think of her co-workers back home as she passed Merlin's sloppy desk. How the man could keep track of anything in this mess was beyond her, and she knew that Sam and Dean would agree. News reporting was a chaotic job all on its own without having to worry about where to find your notepad and pen.

She stopped in front of a shelf stuffed with journalism magazines, the same kind of magazines that her boss, Sam, read with earnest each month.

"Merlin, do you mind if I look through some of these?"

Merlin turned slowly from the window, his eyes hooded and distant.

"Nah, go right ahead."

She pulled three of the most recent issues from the shelves and flipped the first one open, holding it up to the slowly decreasing light from the room's lone window.

The first few articles were written by well known journalists. Each story contained a variety of tips from how to nail down a potential—yet elusive—source, to writing an award-winning lead.

Elise turned the page, her eyes coming to rest on the bold headline:

When a Letter to the Editor is From a Killer
By Lance Donaldson
City Editor, Sandusky News Times

Complainers, pontificators, and ego maniacs have sent their share of letters to the paper during my tenure as city editor at the Sandusky News Times. But never, in all my years, had I received a letter from a killer.

Until now.

Elise's eyes flew through each line of the article, stopping on a copy of the letter that was the catalyst for the editor's piece.

Dear Editor,

For years I have opened my newspaper and seen the faces of people that you, and the rest of the world, deem special. You know the type—the blue ribbon winners, the self-made millionaires, the beauty pageant contestants.

But never have I felt more compelled to say—and do—something until now.

Walter James' article on hard working kids being the "stars" of the future was the final straw. According to Walter James, underachieving kids are the future dregs of society "just as they've been for each previous generation."

But has Mr. James ever looked to the adults surrounding the underachiever for answers?

No, he hasn't.

Because it's easier for him— and all of society—to simply write people off if they don't fit into the desired mold.

I was one of those so-called "underachievers," and in my opinion, the world has more "stars" than it needs. Especially in light of the star-making qualifications dreamed up by the press and accepted as gospel by the rest of the world.

Just because I wasn't a straight-A student or a member of some academic honor society doesn't mean I was an underachiever. Just because I didn't slap a helmet on my head and plow into other kids doesn't mean I was an underachiever. Just because I didn't win a spelling bee or paint my pictures with "happy colors" doesn't mean I was an underachiever. Just because I questioned senseless laws and didn't accept everything thrown at me, doesn't mean I was an underachiever.

But to you it did. To my teachers it did. To the coaches in my school it did. To the police officers on the street it did. To my father, who wrote about my wonderful overachieving counterparts, it did.

Your so-called "pillars of society" are where they are because they stepped on people like me, never looking back to see the face under their foot.

Those "hard working kids" you allude to have gone on to be the teachers and cops and parents who will perpetuate your idea of what a "good kid" is.

Unless I do something to stop it. And you can count on that. I will stop it one "pillar of society" at a time. Starting with those who represent the people who wrote me off.

The first on my list?

A teacher.

Why? Because when I was a kid, I tried to show them who I was inside, and they simply refused to notice me unless I held myself to the measuring stick of their choosing.

And my next victim?

A school counselor.

Why?

For labeling me as a "troubled kid" because it was easy.

And then?

Another pillar.

And another.

One pillar at a time...

~Frank

"Oh my God, Jonathan, this is it!" The article shook with her hand as she looked up from the magazine, her heart thumping in her chest. It was what she'd been hoping for, yet afraid she'd never find.

Within seconds, Jonathan was at her side, grabbing the magazine from her still-trembling hand. His eyes scanned the page and widened as they worked their way down—the intense expression on his face proof that she wasn't dreaming.

"Hey, let me see that, too."

Merlin pushed his way between the shelf and newsroom wall to peer around Jonathan's shoulder, his narrow mouth tightening as his eyes moved rapidly back and forth across the article.

"He's gotta be the guy, don't you think?" She could hear the excitement in her voice, feel the relief in her body as she waited for the men to confirm what she already knew in her heart.

"I'd say so. Nice work, Elise." Jonathan rubbed his right hand across his chin, held the magazine in his left while he waited for Merlin to finish reading. "The fact that a teacher was murdered shortly after this article was received is indication this Frank guy was serious. Toss in the fact that a school counselor died shortly after by someone masquerading as a teacher—and we've got a direct tie-in to the call Mitch and Brad got from Agent Walker."

"Do you think the school counselor was the last victim?"

Jonathan considered her question for a few minutes. "I doubt it. My guess is he's further down the list by now."

"But he doesn't say who the next target is," Elise said, the exasperation in her voice evident to her own ears.

"Not in an obvious way he doesn't. But he definitely left some clues."

Elise scanned the letter again, stopped halfway down the page. "Oh my gosh, you're right. He specifically singled out coaches, police officers—"

"And his dad." Merlin handed the article to Elise, his eyes hooded.

"If only we knew who the last victim was." Elise watched as Merlin jammed his hands into his pockets and headed toward the window once again. Her eyes traveled past the newsman to the darkening skies outside. "If we did, then we'd know who we were looking for now."

"That'd be nice. But at least we have more than we had this morning." Jonathan walked over to the basket where they'd been working for hours. "What I don't get is why there wasn't anything in the wires about this guy."

"I don't get it, either." Elise looked around the newsroom, her gaze stopping on Merlin's paper-strewn desk. "Merlin, do you always put the wire stories into that basket?"

"Yup."

She looked at the desk once again, at the heaps and heaps of paper haphazardly piled across every square inch of surface space. What was it that was bugging her about that desk?

"Elise, I think we should take what we've got and head back to the station now." Jonathan turned toward the window as he pulled his coat on, zipped it to the top. "Thanks for everything, Merlin. We've gotten a lot closer to the killer today."

"That you have. That you have." The newsman turned from the window, the corners of his mouth inched upward as he looked at both of them. "The printed word is powerful. Unfortunately, it's often used in misguided ways."

Elise slipped her arms into her parka and gestured toward the magazine in her left hand. "We're gonna need to take this back to Mitch and Brad so they can see it."

"It's all yours." Merlin crossed the newsroom and walked beside them to the front door. "Let me know if I can be of any further help. And Elise, keep those eyes and ears open for me, will you?"

She smiled and squeezed his dry, cracked hand.

"Absolutely. And you get some rest. You don't need that flu resurfacing."

Merlin waved his hand in the air. "I think that part's over."

Twenty One
7:25 p.m.

HE'D LOVED THE smell of gasoline since he was a kid. In fact, he'd rank it right up there as one of the best smells of all time, second only to a high school lab room on dissection day.

Though, after tonight, he might have to consider swapping their order. After all, gas offered a two-part olfactory experience—its initial form and the resulting odor once ignited.

He set the can down in the snow and reached into his pocket. His fingers closed around the small cardboard sleeve that bore the name *Sophie's Place*. He would have preferred the longer matches, but it really didn't matter. A flame was a flame.

He bent down, twisted the cap to the left, his smile widening as he worked.

Twenty-Two
7:30 p.m.

NOW THAT SHE'D finally made up her mind to tell him, Elise wasn't nervous anymore. Maybe it was because it was necessary—to ensure Uncle Ken's safety. Maybe it was because she wanted to believe their relationship was strong enough to withstand a difference of opinion.

Or was it?

She pulled the eyelet quilt around her shoulders and sunk into the floral loveseat, pulling her legs underneath her body. Mitch looked so pensive as he poked at the crackling fire, his face illuminated by the ensuing sparks. He was so strong, so smart, so good looking. But he'd had a tough life because of his dad's murder. And the fact that the criminal escaped hard time with an insanity plea had made Mitch ultra sensitive to what he saw as cracks in the justice system.

She'd just have to hope he'd be open to the possibility that some deaths could truly be an accident. Like Aunt Faye's.

"Come sit with me, Mitch."

She met his soft brown eyes with a smile, patted the vacant spot on the loveseat.

He placed the poker in the rack with the other fireplace tools and sat down beside her.

"You did really good today, Elise." Mitch pushed a renegade curl from her face and kissed her firmly on the mouth. "That article really helps us get in this guy's mindset."

Elise burrowed into his chest as his arm draped across her shoulder, pulling her close.

"I'm glad it helped. I just wish we could've found something in the wire stories that might help us follow his trail a little better."

She stared at the flames as they leapt from the logs, noticed the way their tear-drop shape seemed etched in blue.

This was what Elise had envisioned for their trip. Quiet nights curled up in front of the fire, nestling.

"What you *did* find is better than what we had."

She tilted her head upward, kissed the bottom of his stubbly chin. "I know. But I want to find more." She grimaced at the rough feel of his unshaven face as she kissed his chin once again. "But I think there's still a chance I will."

"How's that?" Mitch linked his arms around her back and brushed her forehead with his lips.

"Let's just say that Merlin isn't what you'd call tidy. I'm kinda hoping he'll let me organize his desk after being down with the flu for so long."

"That's good. Maybe he left a few of those wire stories on his desk and he just missed it."

She looked at the golden flecks in Mitch's eyes, studied the way they sparkled in the firelight. "That's what I'm hoping for."

Mitch cleared his throat, kissed her forehead, her eyes. "I'm sorry our trip turned out like this. It's not the way I wanted to spend our time alone."

"It's okay. It can't be helped."

She nestled against his chest once again, stared at the crackling fire in the grate. If she could just get started, the words would come. But it was the getting started part that was the hardest.

"Mitch?"

"Uh huh?"

"Um, I...uh..." Elise squeezed her eyes shut for a moment, listened to his heart beating against her ear. "So you really feel good about the kid at the livery?"

She was such a coward.

"Yeah, I do. Seemed to be a real honest, gentle kid who just wants to reconnect with someone but lost the nerve once he got here."

Elise considered Mitch's words. She knew about wanting to reconnect with someone. And in a way she had. The only problem now was telling Mitch about it.

She startled as a log suddenly split in two, sending sparks flying.

"Hey. You're okay." Mitch tightened his arms around her. "I know things aren't normal right now, but you've got to trust that I'm gonna do everything in my power to keep you safe."

She swallowed over the sudden lump in her throat, caused by guilt, no doubt. Guilt that she could keep a secret from a man who put her first. Always.

She reached for the heart-shaped locket around her neck, moved it back and forth along the delicate gold chain. It was now or never.

"Mitch, I've got to tell you someth—"

Muffled shouts from the hallway cut her sentence short. She jumped to her feet.

"Oh my God, what now?" Elise sprinted across the room with Mitch at her heels, yanked open the door to the hallway.

"Fire! Fire!"

A woman in her mid-sixties was running down the hall toward the staircase, screaming the same word over and over.

Elise inhaled deeply, sniffed the air for any indication of smoke. But there was none.

"Excuse me, ma'am?" Elise said, as she jogged down the kerosene-lit hallway. "Where's the fire?"

The woman grabbed hold of Elise's arm, her eyes filled with fear. "The building. Down the road. It's on fire." She pointed toward her open doorway on the other side of the hallway. "Go look."

Elise followed behind Mitch as he ran into the woman's room and stopped just inside the doorway. A bright orange glow lit the corner of the hotel room closest to the window.

Flames shot toward the sky, illuminating the night. And even though she didn't know the island well, there was no doubt which building was on fire.

"Oh, dear God, it's Merlin's place!"

11:50 p.m.

ELISE STARED AT the water-soaked shell as it smoldered in the darkness, swallowed around the sooty film that filled her throat.

The whole thing felt surreal. A nightmare on top of a nightmare. Only she wasn't dreaming.

She pulled Jonathan's parka tightly around her chest, grateful for his generosity. Neither she nor Mitch had thought of anything other than the fire as they ran out of the hotel and into the cold, night air.

But now, standing here, it seemed ludicrous to think they could have done anything to help. Half of the building was engulfed in flames when they reached it, the heat of the fire enough to warm their frigid bodies. Until now.

She strained to see Mitch or Brad's outline against the lingering smoke. It drove her crazy thinking they were walking around in the smoldering building, searching.

Elise swiped at the tear that rolled down her cheek. What she wouldn't give to have Merlin tap her on the shoulder right now. But as each second passed, the likelihood of that happening grew smaller and smaller.

"You okay, Elise?"

"I can't believe he's gone, Jonathan. We were just with him this afternoon." Her voice trailed off as she looked at the building. What was left of it, anyway.

"I know."

"I got a little nervous that first day. The way he had all those candles so close to the paper stacks. But I didn't want to offend him by commenting on it." She closed her eyes and continued. "What an idiot I am."

"This isn't your fault, Elise. When an accelerant is used, it doesn't matter whether you've got a candle burning or stacks of paper covering every square inch. All you need is a single match to make it go."

The enormity of his words washed over her like ice water. "Someone *did* this to him?"

Jonathan nodded, his eyes unreadable. "Yep."

"But how do you know that?"

"We found an empty gas can and a book of matches in the back."

"But who would want to..."

She stopped, stared at the lingering smoke. She really didn't need to finish the question. They both knew that. The answer was simple.

Instead, she forced her mouth to form another useless question.

"But why?"

Jonathan stuffed his hands into his pockets and looked toward the rising smoke. "My guess? We got too close to the truth today with that article you found."

"And Merlin?" Elise asked.

"He was expendable."

Jonathan's words hovered in the air, their meaning pressing down on them with an intensity she couldn't deny. It was all so sad. So incredibly sad.

She closed her eyes, felt Jonathan's hands gently rubbing her shoulders. His quiet understanding was exactly what she needed.

A snap of wood made them both jump and she squinted into the remains of the building. Mitch's tall, muscular form came into sight, Brad's stockier outline just a few steps behind.

"We found him. He was in his bed."

Monday, January 31st
Twenty-Three
3:00 a.m.

NO MATTER HOW many times they verbally walked through Merlin's office building, Mitch still couldn't shake the feeling that they had missed something. Something big.

"There's gotta be something in that building that'll point to the killer, something he left behind, something he didn't cover well enough." Mitch stretched his arms above his head and yawned. His body ached all over from holding the heavy fire hose, yet his mind refused to shut down for the night. The killer was becoming increasingly more desperate and that could only mean one thing. The guy was about to get sloppy. And when he did, Mitch would be waiting.

"Christ, Mitch, what could we have missed? There's nothing left except scorched lumber and a boatload of ashes." Brad leaned his head against the wall, his eyes drooped. "And if I don't get some sleep soon, I'm gonna be useless."

Mitch made eye contact with Jonathan from across the room, recognized the smirk on the retired cop's face.

Gonna be useless?

"Maybe tomorrow, when it's light out, you'll find something."

Mitch turned and looked at Elise. She seemed so tired, so sad, her voice barely audible. She was taking Merlin's death hard.

He crossed the room and took her hand in his.

"You okay, hon?"

143

"I will be."

He hated to see the tears that welled in her eyes, hated the fact that she'd grown so fond of Merlin only to have him fall prey to a psychopath.

"I'm gonna catch this guy, Elise."

She squeezed his hand gently, her trembling voice a near whisper. "I know you will, Mitch. I'm just worried about..."

He saw the pain in her face as her voice faltered and trailed off. Something was weighing on her. He'd felt it since the afternoon they arrived.

"Worried about what?"

She touched his face, her soft hand sending a jolt through his body.

"Worried about you. Me. Everyone."

He pulled her close. "We're getting closer. I can feel it."

"I agree." Jonathan pushed off Mitch's bed and stood. "I think Elise and I got too close for comfort with that magazine article. And I'd bet good money that we were close to finding a picture he didn't want us to find."

"That's exactly what I've been thinking." Mitch rubbed Elise's arm as he continued. "He set that fire out of desperation. And desperate people make mistakes."

He studied Jonathan's face in the firelight and saw the set to his jaw, the tension in his stance. It was a welcomed look Mitch recognized all to well. It was the look of determination. A look he'd pay good money to get from Brad.

Mitch swung his gaze onto his college buddy, felt the quick ripple of anger course through his body as he realized Brad was asleep.

So much for unified determination.

Twenty-Four
10:00 a.m.

"COME IN. COME in. You've all had such a long night."

Mitch peered over Elise's head and managed a smile. "Morning, Sophie."

The woman pulled a cloth from her pocket and quickly wiped the already-gleaming table that had become "theirs" over the past few days. "You poor things, you look like you've had no sleep."

Mitch pulled Elise's chair out, waited for her to sit. "I think we got a few hours, right guys?"

"Yeah, probably about four or so." Jonathan unzipped his parka and draped it over the back of his chair.

"Maybe you got four, man, but I slept like crap on Mitch's damn floor."

Elise reached out and patted Sophie's hand. "We did fine. Really."

Mitch studied Elise's drawn face, saw the exhaustion in her eyes yet marveled at the way she seemed to stay so cheerful to those around her. It was one of the many things he'd grown to love about her over the past seven months.

"So what'll it be everyone?"

Mitch sat back in his chair, listened as Jonathan and Brad took turns ordering everything from coffee and eggs, to oatmeal and hot tea. Anything that could possibly appear on the table warm, compliments of Sophie's propane stove. When it was Elise's turn, her quiet voice made his heart ache for the trip they'd envisioned.

145

"How about you, Mitch?"

He didn't know how he was going to swing it, but he was gonna save every penny he could once they got back to Jersey—just so he could take her on a real vacation. Sans serial killers of course.

"Mitch?"

"What? Oh, sorry, Sophie. I'll just take some coffee."

"Comin' right up." Sophie turned and headed toward the kitchen, stopped just before the swinging door that separated the dining area from the backroom where she cooked. "Oh, and Mitch? Your friend, the redhead? He was looking for you a little while ago. Said he had something important to show you."

"Mark?"

"Yeah, that's him. He was real agitated. Not that I can blame him with the way that one skier is always following him. I tell you, *that* one is bad news."

"Who?"

Sophie pointed to the picture of the orienteering group, her finger coming to rest on a short squatty guy hamming it up in the front row.

"Josh Cummings? Why do you say he's bad news?" Mitch asked.

"Well, maybe bad news is a little harsh. But my gut says he's slimy."

Mitch nodded as he looked at the picture. "Do you know what it was that Mark wanted to show me?"

"Nope. We got sidetracked on the fire. He was upset that he hadn't heard about it."

Mitch straightened in his chair.

"Why was he upset about that?"

"He's a firefighter. He said he could've helped."

"That's right. I forgot about that. He would know a lot about fires then, wouldn't he?"

Mitch didn't wait for a response to his question. He pushed his chair back and stood, placed a hand on Brad's shoulder.

"C'mon Brad, we gotta go find Mark. See what he wants once and for all."

"But my coffee. My eggs."

"You'll survive, Brad." Mitch grabbed his coat. "Elise, are you okay staying here with Jonathan and Sophie?"

"Yes. Now go find Mark."

She looked across the table at Sophie's gently lined face and saw the concerned eyes that studied her in return.

"And Merlin? He's really gone?"

Elise nodded slowly.

She was grateful when Jonathan finally took control of the conversation, providing the details that were simply too painful to relate.

"Mitch and Brad found his body. He was in his bed when the fire happened. They think he probably died from inhalation."

Sophie made a soft *tsking* sound under her breath as she fiddled with the handkerchief in her hand. "It's just so hard to fathom, his being gone. Merlin's been a staple on this island for as long as I've been here. Nearly twenty years, I'd say. He always said the island was the best of both worlds—a chance to tell the news and a place to escape family."

"Escape family?" Jonathan took a sip of his coffee, then set the mug down on the table. "That's a rather odd thing to say."

"I thought so, too," Sophie said. "But I never pressed. I always found it strange how much he liked to report the news, yet how reticent he was to talk about himself."

"That's par for the course with most writers. They like to write, not talk," Elise said quietly. "He was a true newsman—always asking me questions. And the way he went after you, Jonathan, when we told him you were a cop. Wow."

Jonathan chuckled.

"You're a police officer, too, Jonathan?"

Surprised, Elise looked at the woman. "You didn't know that, Sophie?"

"No."

Jonathan straightened in his chair. "I guess we've tried to keep that fact quiet so I could be privy to things I might not otherwise hear."

Elise saw the corners of Sophie's mouth tug upward, her eyes sparkle momentarily.

"The Lord has been watching out for us this week. How else could you explain your presence?" Sophie brushed a piece of hair from her forehead and leaned back in her seat. "To have four police officers at a time like this is nothing short of a blessing."

"*Three* police officers," Elise gently corrected as she slid her hand between her mug and its handle.

The woman's brows furrowed in confusion.

"No, four. Mitch, Brad, Jonathan, and your other friend."

Elise pushed her mug aside. It worried her to see the woman so distracted, confused. "There isn't any other friend. Mitch and I are here by ourselves."

Sophie slid her hand across the table and raised it to her head, moved her fingers in a small massaging motion at her temple. "Didn't you have someone with you that first night at dinner?"

"No. Just us. As a matter of fact, Mitch and I were the only ones in the restaurant that first night. No, wait, that's not quite right, either. There was that one lone soul who came in looking as if he'd been out in the cold for hours."

"I guess you'd know better than I if you'd been sitting with someone else that night." Sophie closed her eyes momentarily. "I don't think I've ever felt as scatterbrained as I have this week. I guess it's just stress."

Jonathan shoveled his spoon around the bowl in an attempt to get every last drop of oatmeal. "Stress'll do that to you."

Elise nodded and leaned back in her seat.

"Did you ever come across that picture of Mark, Sophie?"

"No. But I know I took one." She peered at Elise from behind her glasses. "But there's another picture I'd like you to see."

"Oh?"

"Wait right here."

Sophie rose from her chair and headed toward the counter in the far right corner of the restaurant.

"I wonder how Mitch and Brad are faring with our pal, Mark," Jonathan said.

Elise shrugged. "I can't figure out what he's so anxious to show Mitch."

"I can't figure that one out, either." Jonathan took a last sip of coffee and then pushed his empty mug into the middle of the table.

Elise felt a hand on her shoulder and turned. Sophie stood behind her, a photograph clutched in her right hand.

"Oh Sophie, how'd you develop our picture in this storm? You've got way too much to be worrying about right now."

Sophie gently stroked Elise's hair. "This isn't your picture from the other night. That's still sitting in the roll on top of the counter."

"Then what is that?"

Sophie eased herself into the chair beside Elise. "I started the picture wall fifteen years ago. Have taken a picture of every person or group that's been in here since then."

Curious, Elise watched as Sophie continued to grasp the photograph in her right hand, quietly clenching and unclenching her left.

"I know. You told us that the first night. It's a wonderful id—"

"And once a picture's up, it stays up," Sophie said quickly.

"You said that, too, though I don't know how you can fit fifteen years worth of photographs on these walls." Elise scanned the restaurant quickly, then brought her gaze back to rest on Sophie.

"Well, they might not always be on the walls—but I always have them out somewhere."

"Okay."

Sophie slowly turned the photograph over and placed it on the table in front of Elise.

Elise looked down at the image, felt her stomach drop as her eyes focused on the happy foursome peering back at her.

11:00 a.m.

MITCH STAMPED THE snow from his boots as he walked across the entry foyer toward the registration desk. The Lakeside Inn looked very different in the morning light, less cozy. But maybe that's because the last time he walked through the front door he had no idea that a woman had been strangled to death behind the same counter where Tom now stood. "Hey there, Tom, how ya holding up?"

"If people didn't care about things like warm water and electricity, it wouldn't be so bad." The young man ran a sleeve across his brow and continued. "But, since they do, it's not exactly smooth sailing."

Brad snorted. "I can imagine. But hey, buddy, if you want to trade jobs for the next few weeks, I'm game."

Mitch looked quickly at the ceiling and tried not to dwell on the idea that a twenty-year-old hotel clerk would probably do a better job than Brad.

"I'd love to do what you do, Brad. Too bad trading ain't an option."

Too bad, indeed.

"Can you tell me what room Mark Tallberg is staying in?" Mitch asked.

"I'm not really supposed to give that information out. Unless there's some police reason..." Tom looked at Mitch, excitement crackling behind his eyes.

"I was told he's been looking for me. Has something important to tell me. I mean, *show* me."

"Oh yeah, I remember that. He was muttering under his breath when he walked back in here about an hour ago. Complaining that you're never where you're supposed to be."

Mitch set his elbow on the countertop and leaned in toward Tom. "Well, I'm here now."

"Okay. I just hope it doesn't get me fired."

"It won't."

Mitch watched as Tom strode across the small office area and reached for the guest book they'd looked through just three days earlier.

"I should know this guy's room by heart. I put his prize money in the safe just like he asked, yet he still checks on it almost hourly." Tom flipped the book open, ran his index finger down the page. "Here we go, room 327."

The clerk set the book down and pointed toward the stairs just beyond the hearth room. "Go up to the third floor. Mr. Tallberg's room will be four doors down on the left."

Mitch tapped the top of the counter quickly. "Thanks, man." He turned in the direction of the staircase and stopped. "What are you waiting for, Brad? Let's go."

He took the stairs two at a time as he headed toward the third floor, Brad in tow.

"This better be good," Brad mumbled under his breath as they rounded the second floor landing and continued on. Mitch chose to ignore Brad, to focus on the task at hand. Mark's desire to talk to him was intriguing. He just hoped it paid off with something important.

When they reached the third floor landing, he half-jogged down the hall, searching for the correct door.

"Here we go. Room 327." He raised his fist and pounded. "Mark?"

The door jerked open.

"Detective Burns! I've been looking for you. I've got something you need to see."

"I heard. That's why I'm here."

"Good. C'mon in." Mark stepped to the side to allow Mitch and Brad to enter the room.

"So what's this about, Mark?" Mitch strode over to the window and turned, his hand resting on his holster.

"This!" Mark pulled a round black object from his chest of drawers. "It was Pete's."

Mitch reached for the high tech compass that Mark held out, flipped it over in his hands.

"How'd you get this?"

"I was in the hearth room the other night, trying to warm up after skiing, and I bumped into that idiot, Josh."

"Josh?"

Mitch looked quickly at Brad. "Josh. Josh Cummings. He's one of the orienteering club members. The one with the temper."

"Temper? That's putting it lightly. The guy's a first class idiot." Mark squared his shoulders and puffed out his chest. "He basically attacked me when I won the competition. Kept telling me I must have cheated. And instead of getting on *him*, the other guys starting laying into me. Told me to walk away from him."

Mitch looked down at the compass again, turned it over in his hands, studied every inch of the tool. A tool that Josh was convinced would have made the difference between winning and losing the orienteering competition.

"I'd have won with that compass."

"Anyway, he comes over to me the other night like he'd done nothing wrong. Like we were best buds or something," Mark continued. "I didn't want to cause a scene in front of the other guests who were huddled around the fire, so I tried my best to ignore him."

Mitch looked up. "Then what?"

"He tells me he needs gloves, that he lost his somewhere. Told me his hands were getting frostbite." Mark crossed his arms in front of his chest. "But you know what? They didn't have that red and puffy look skin gets when it's been exposed to the elements."

"And?"

"He asked me if I had an extra pair of gloves to spare. I told him no. But some poor slob next to me offered him a pair."

Mitch ran his hand across his eyes and over his hair, waited for Mark to get to the compass part but knew better than to rush an interview.

"Josh said he didn't like to take charity so he gave the guy a compass in return." Mark pointed to the compass in Mitch's hand. "That compass."

"So how'd you get it?" Brad stretched his arms above his head and yawned.

"As soon as Josh headed up to his room, I asked the guy if I could see the compass. Recognized it as Pete's right away. He'd shown it to me that first morning. It's top of the line. It even has two second dampening."

"Two second dampening? What's that?" Brad asked.

"It's the time it takes for the compass needle to settle. Most take at least four. It gives you a two second advantage every time you take a reading," Mitch explained.

"Very good, Detective." Mark said. "Anyway, as soon as I got my hands on that compass my antennae went up."

Mitch studied Mark's face, looked for any indication he was trying to pull something. But he saw nothing that raised suspicion.

"Keep going."

"I saw Josh in the lobby the next morning and asked him about the compass. He acted like I had two heads, insisted he didn't know what I was talking about."

Mitch stared at Mark. "You mean he pretended he hadn't traded the compass the night before?"

"You got it. But that's not all. He actually said Pete's senseless death was on my neck."

"What?"

"He said Pete's death was senseless—because of me."

Mitch closed his eyes briefly, recalled the conversation he'd had with Dan Friar the morning of the search.

"His name's Josh. Got real pissy when Mark won yesterday. Started cursing and kicking at the snow. It was really kind of funny."

Mitch opened his eyes.

"...he was hollerin' about his ex-wife and how she was draining him..."

Was it possible that Josh had murdered Pete in an effort to win?

Mitch thought back to the interview with Josh. The way he'd been adamant about the compass being the difference between winning and losing.

If he'd killed Pete, stolen the compass, and *still* lost, he'd be outraged. Killing Pete would have been for nothing.

He looked at Mark. "How did he phrase that statement about Pete's death again?"

"He said Pete's death was senseless—because of me."

Bingo!

He raised his hand to his mouth, pulled it across his lips. During his interview with Josh and Dan, Josh had said he had what he needed to win. And he believed the compass was Pete's magic bullet.

But if Josh *had* killed Pete, why would he have killed Annie? And Merlin?

Unless...

"Do you know where Josh is now?"

Mark nodded. "Holed up in his room down the hall."

Mitch ran through the host of scenarios playing in his head. If his gut was right, Josh was a one-timer and, therefore, the lesser of two evils.

"Can you help me out, Mark?"

"What do you need?"

"Can you keep an eye on Josh? Make sure he doesn't stray too far?"

Mark pushed off the wall. "I can do that if you want. But I can also help investigate that fire last night, too."

"I'll let you know on the fire, but right now I need the help with Josh." Mitch patted the redhead's shoulder as he headed toward the door. "Brad, let's go."

"Where are we going now?"

"Merlin's," Mitch snapped.

When they stepped into the hallway and pulled Mark's door shut behind them, Brad stopped. "What's going on, Mitch?"

Mitch lowered his voice to a near-whisper. "Pete Garner wasn't a victim of the serial killer. Annie and Merlin were."

"Huh?"

"We're dealing with two different killers, Brad."

11:00 a.m.

"OH, ELISE, I didn't want this picture to cause you pain. I just wanted you to know that I know." Sophie's hand moved across Elise's back in a wide circle.

"Who is that?"

Elise raised her head just enough to look into Jonathan's bewildered face.

"That's me," she said, her voice quiet and raspy.

"You?" Jonathan gently turned the photograph just enough that he could see the faces more clearly.

"Yes."

"You were young."

She nodded. "I was nine."

"Is that your parents and your brother?"

"No. That's my aunt and uncle. And my cousin, Ray."

"Did something happen to them?"

She traced her aunt's outline with her finger. "About a year after this was taken. Aunt Faye died at home."

Her eyes focused on little Ray—his beaming face and ocean-blue eyes. He'd been such a nice kid. A gentle old soul trapped in a child's body.

"How?"

The words poured from her mouth, their meaning hollow to her own ears. "My Uncle Ken had a hotrod he was restoring in the garage. He'd been messing with it before he left for work. He forgot to turn it off."

Jonathan spoke, his voice quiet, yet strong. "Carbon monoxide poisoning?"

"Yes."

He sighed. "Poor guy. I bet his life's been hell since then."

"He's made sure of that," Elise whispered.

"What do you mean?"

"My whole family. Faye's whole family. They all turned against him. Said his negligence was unforgivable. No one realized that their lack of forgiveness didn't come close to his feelings toward himself."

"What happened to him?"

"He's here. On Mackinac," Sophie interjected in a hushed voice.

"Is that what you've been keeping from Mitch?" Jonathan asked quietly.

Elise nodded.

"But why?"

She squeezed her eyes tightly against the tears. "Mitch's dad was murdered when Mitch was in high school. It took years for the cops to find his killer. When they finally did, the guy pleaded insanity and bypassed jail time. That's what's made Mitch so passionate about people paying for their crimes. It's why he became a cop. Normally I agree with his views, but in this case, I don't. I'm not sure I want that between us."

Silence blanketed the tiny restaurant momentarily as Elise continued to cry. There was nothing they could say.

Finally, Jonathan spoke. "And the boy? Was he in the house, too?"

"No. Thank God. He was at a friend's house that day," said Elise, sniffling. "His grandparents invoked their guardianship since Ken was not little Ray's real father. Said they couldn't trust someone so negligent with a child."

Jonathan sighed. "Man, he paid for his mistake, didn't he?"

"In spades. He loved Faye. Loved little Ray. He wanted nothing more than to spend the rest of his life loving them. And I truly believe that losing them was his punishment for being careless. And he's had to live with that knowledge every day since. I can't imagine a worse hell."

Twenty-Five
1:30 p.m.

THE REMNANTS OF the newspaper building crackled under his feet as Mitch walked carefully through the area that was once the heart and soul of the Island News. A metal desk was one of the only identifiable objects that remained in this area, the deep piles of ash indicative of the wall-to-wall paper stacks Elise had described after her first visit.

"See that right there? That's where he started the fire," Mitch said, pointing at a v-pattern near the base of the north outer wall. "That's a pour mark from the gasoline he used to start it."

"How do you know so damn much, Mitch?" Brad asked, squatting down for a closer look.

"I took a class on arson investigation about a year ago. The chief thought it was a good idea to get me up and trained in case we needed it one day."

"Have you had to use it much?"

"I haven't used it at all. Until today."

Brad straightened up. "This room was just an inferno waiting to happen. I don't think Merlin ever threw away a paper. He used to say that preserving the history of the island was up to him."

Mitch coughed. The smell of smoke still clung to everything in the building as well as to the air around it. "I'm sure all that paper made it burn faster and hotter, but with that gasoline and a wood building—it was gonna go. Regardless."

Brad stepped gingerly across a board. "I don't think there's much left to find in here."

"It doesn't hurt to look around, though. Turn things over, open some drawers." Mitch stepped across a hole in the floor and headed toward the south side of the building. "I'm gonna take a look around Merlin's room. Maybe I'll find something in the daylight that we didn't spot last night."

Mitch slowly picked his way over to the room where Merlin's body had been found. They'd gotten to the fire before this area had been totally destroyed, but had been too late to save a sleeping Merlin from smoke inhalation.

His eyes lingered on the bed, on the spot where they'd found Merlin's body. He inhaled deeply and willed his mind not to think of the late night burial under the snow. It was the part of police work that he hated. But when he could find answers and offer justice to the loved ones left behind, his choice of career was more than worth it.

A small metal box inside a doorway caught his eye. A fire box.

He jiggled the handle, prayed it was unlocked. But it wasn't. His gaze skirted across what was left of Merlin's dresser and came to rest on a sooty object beside the bed.

A key ring.

Mitch separated each individual key from the next until he came to a small key that looked to be about the right size. He slid it carefully into the lock and twisted, grinned at the catch sound.

"Ta-da."

He flipped the lid back and looked inside. A passport, birth certificate, social security card, and other personal papers just about filled the entire box.

He reached inside, removed each paper one at a time. At the bottom of the box he found a small wallet-size album.

Closing his hand around the soft leather, Mitch rose slowly and headed back toward Brad.

As they rounded the corner, Mitch saw someone waiting under the station's front overhang.

"Who's that?" Brad asked.

"Looks like Mark."

They pushed forward with their ski poles until they reached the base of the front step.

"Hey, Mark. Did something come up with Josh?" Mitch unsnapped his boots and stepped onto the porch.

"Nah. Talked to the kid at the front desk. He said Josh called down for something to help him sleep. Seems he was awake all night tossin' and turnin'. Guess killing someone will do that to you." Mark rubbed his gloved hands together. "So, thanks to whatever the kid gave him, he's out cold. And I—"

"What?"

"Well, I sort of barricaded his door to make sure he couldn't go anywhere before I got back."

"I didn't hear that, okay?" Mitch unlocked the station door with the spare key Brad had loaned him and pushed the door open. "C'mon in for a minute."

"You guys look beat," Mark said as he followed Mitch into the station.

"We just spent the past hour picking through a burned out building." Brad peeled off his coat, dropped it on the chair in the waiting area, and headed toward the window behind his desk.

"Geez, Brad, can't you just leave the damn thing shut for once?" Mitch shook his head as he watched his friend unlock the window and raise it about a foot.

"If you want me to stay awake, you're gonna have to deal with the window." Brad dropped into his chair and kicked his feet up onto the desk.

"I keep mine open, too—even in the winter," Mark said. "Only for me, I like the window open so I can listen to the outdoors."

Mitch turned and looked at Mark. "Listen to the outdoors?"

"Yeah. You'd be amazed at the sounds you hear outside—even in a blizzard like this."

Mitch dropped into the extra desk chair and pushed a pen around his legal pad, pondering Mark's words as his gaze stopped on Brad's open window.

"I like the window open so I can listen."

Listen.

Mitch jumped up, ran to the window, looked outside at the large tree that provided an excellent shield for anyone who might be standing outside.

Near the window.

He turned slowly from the window and slammed his fist against the wall. "Damn it!"

Brad pulled his feet from the desk, his face contorted with confusion. "What's wrong?"

"Your window, Brad. Your *open* window." He didn't know why it hadn't dawned on him before now. It made perfect sense.

"What about my window?"

"Haven't you found it odd how the killer seemed to know things?"

"Like..."

"Like Annie and the fact that she could identify him. Like the fact that Merlin's office might hold a key to his identity. For God sake, how stupid could we be?"

"What are you saying?" Brad asked.

Mitch held his hand in front of his eyes as he spoke. "The killer has known almost every move we've made."

"How?"

"He was listening. Outside your window."

Brad dropped his head onto his desk as a string of obscenities filled the room.

"I'M GONNA HEAD back to the hotel, make sure that loser is still sleeping." Mark grabbed for his parka and stood. "What do you want me to do if he leaves the hotel?"

Mitch moved his fist to the side of his mouth long enough to speak. "Follow him."

"You got it."

He watched as Mark headed for the door, determination in the man's eyes. "Hey, Mark?"

"Yeah?"

"Jonathan's a cop."

"Jonathan? The guy from my hotel?"

"Yeah. We needed to keep that to ourselves for a while. Sorry."

Mark shrugged.

"I'm gonna be sending him over to pick up Josh shortly."

"Okay. Can I stay with them, see this through? For Pete?"

Mitch nodded, ashamed of his faulty character assessment where Mark was concerned. "Sure."

Mark raised his hand in a salute and yanked the outer door open, a swirl of cold air rushing to fill the open space.

"Do you think we can really count on him with this?"

Mitch shifted his gaze from the closing door, to Brad, willed himself to keep his frustration in check. Brad's weird obsession with fresh air had given the killer the upper hand the last few days and forced Mitch to have to rely on the help of others.

"We've got no other choice, Brad. We've got a skier who was killed for money by a desperate guy who more than likely snapped in the moment. And then we've got a serial killer roaming the island who's picking off people who threaten him. You tell me which one we need to concentrate on now." His words were curt and angry, but he couldn't hide his frustration any longer.

Speechless, Brad dropped his head back onto his desk.

Mitch resisted the urge to continue, resisted the desire to accuse Brad of stupidity. It wouldn't solve anything.

He grabbed for the album he'd placed on his desk, ran his hand across the soft leather.

Merlin had died at the hand of a psychopath. Someone who couldn't face his own inadequacies.

Mitch flipped the cover open, stared at the face of Merlin Webber that peered back at him from the Michiganissued driver's license. A document that undoubtedly found its way into the album as a sort of keepsake. What other use could it serve on an island with no cars?

His gaze hovered on the man's piercing brown eyes, the thick crop of grey hair. This was the way he wanted to remember the man he'd never met. Not as a corpse being buried in the snow.

Mitch turned the album page and studied the next picture. Dark brown eyes stared back at him, serious eyes that held little joy.

"Who's that?"

Mitch raised his eyes momentarily, met Brad's. "I don't know."

Brad pushed back his chair and joined Mitch.

"That's gotta be Merlin when he was a little younger." Brad leaned over Mitch's shoulder. "Yup, that's Merlin. Grumpy face and all."

Mitch slipped the picture out of its clear plastic sleeve and turned it over. A date was written in the upper right hand corner.

"Wow. Merlin sure aged over the last ten years," Brad snorted.

"How long have you been here again?" Mitch asked.

"About five years."

"Hey boys, what's going on around here?"

Startled, Mitch looked up. "Hey, Jonathan. I didn't hear you come in."

"I could tell. You guys looked pretty engrossed just now."

Mitch motioned to a chair across from his desk, waited for Jonathan to sit.

"Where's Elise?"

"She wanted to stay and talk to Sophie. I figured she could use that," Jonathan said. "So, what'd I miss? What happened with Mark?"

Mitch set the album down. "You missed a lot. The first victim, Pete, had a very high-tech compass he was using during the competition. Mark heard Josh Cummings trading it with a guest at the Lakeside Inn for a pair of gloves the other night. Then, when Mark asked him about it the next morning, Josh denied the whole incident."

He saw the light bulb go off in Jonathan's head, was grateful for the keen instincts the retired police officer still possessed.

"Do you think he—"

"I sure do. It jibes with what Dan told me the morning of the search party. It jibes with the way Mark was so worried about his money. And it jibes with Dan's belief that Pete's killer had to have been a strong skier."

"Then where is he?"

"At his hotel. Asleep."

Jonathan dropped into the chair. "Come again?"

"We've got other fish to fry. Bigger fish."

"Meaning?"

"Meaning Pete's murder was a one-time snap for a pathetic fool who isn't going anywhere in this storm. I'd stake my life on that. But we've got a bigger threat that needs our full attention."

He could see the question in Jonathan's eyes, feel it in the man's demeanor.

"I think Josh is one of *two* killers. It's the other killer that's taking out residents of this island. And it's this other killer that the F.B.I. is tracking."

Mitch paused for a moment then continued. "And we think we've figured out how he's been able to keep a step ahead of us. How he's known to target Annie. And Merlin."

"How?" Jonathan asked.

Brad pushed against the wall with a thud. "Me."

Jonathan's voice was gruff when he spoke. "You?"

"My window."

A low whistle escaped Jonathan's mouth. "Crap! Why didn't we think of that?"

Mitch recognized the frustration in Jonathan's face. But they both were smart enough to know that dwelling wasn't going to solve anything. Moving forward would.

Mitch set Merlin's picture down on the desk and reached for the pad of paper he'd been jotting notes on all week.

Jonathan reached across the desk, turned the photograph in his direction.

"Where'd you get this picture of Merlin?"

"From an album. I found it in a fire box in his bedroom. Thought maybe it would help somehow."

He scanned his notes, reviewing and discarding various scenarios he'd been playing with since that first night.

"That's kinda odd."

Mitch forced his attention away from his notes and onto Jonathan, saw the man furrow his brow as he looked at the picture more closely.

"What?"

"Merlin. Why would he shave his head? It makes him look so much older."

Mitch stared at Jonathan, waited for an explanation for his odd statement. But there was none.

"Merlin's head wasn't shaved."

"Yeah, it was."

Mitch turned and looked at Brad standing behind him, saw the look of confusion in his buddy's face. He turned back to Jonathan.

"Merlin *wasn't* bald. He had a thick crop of grey hair. The same grey hair that was on the body Brad and I buried."

"Maybe he was wearing a wig?"

"Merlin? Wear a wig? Not likely," Brad said, chuckling under his breath.

"What did this bald guy look like?" Mitch asked, Jonathan's words beginning to form an unsettling image in his mind.

"Just like that." Jonathan pointed to the picture on the desk in front of them. "Except bald."

Mitch pushed his chair back and jumped to his feet. "Brad, was that Merlin we buried under the snow?"

"Sure was."

Mitch smacked his hand on the desk top. "Then that wasn't Merlin that you and Elise talked to! That must have been our guy."

"But *this* is Merlin, isn't it?" Jonathan pulled the picture from the desk and held it up in Brad's direction.

"Yup. That's Merlin. A younger version, anyway."

"Well, this is the guy Elise and I met. I'm sure of that."

Mitch stared at Jonathan, his thoughts racing a mile a minute. How could they be referring to the same man? A man they both saw within the last few days?

On impulse, Mitch crossed the room and yanked the file cabinet open. He pulled the journalism magazine from the top drawer, flipped it open to the article Elise had found and began reading the letter to the editor the killer had written.

The letter had been of interest from the beginning, but now parts leapt out at him as if they'd been written in bold print.

> *...Walter James' article on hard working kids being the "stars" of the future was the final straw. According to Walter James, underachieving kids are the future dregs of society "just as they've been for each previous generation."*
>
> *But has Mr. James ever looked to the adults surrounding the underachiever for answers? No he hasn't.*

Mitch's hand tightened on the magazine as his eyes continued to scan the letter.

> *...I was one of those so-called "underachievers," and in my opinion the world has more "stars" than it needs. Especially in light of the star-making qualifications dreamed up by*

the press and accepted as gospel by the rest of the world.

Just because I wasn't a straight-A student or a member of some academic honor society doesn't mean I was an underachiever. Just because I didn't slap a helmet on my head and plow into other kids doesn't mean I was an underachiever. Just because I didn't win a spelling bee or paint my pictures with "happy colors" doesn't mean I was an underachiever...

...But to you it did. To my teachers it did. To the coaches in my school it did. To the police officers on the street it did. To my father, who wrote about my wonderful overachieving counterparts, it did.

"To my father, who *wrote* about my wonderful overachieving counterparts," Mitch's hushed voice trailed off as he reread the last sentence. "That's it!"

"What?" Brad asked.

"The man we buried was Merlin."

"Okay. I knew that."

"The man you saw, Jonathan, wasn't Merlin. It was his son." He stared at Jonathan across the room, saw the frightening realization creep across the man's tired face.

For a moment the station was silent, not a word was spoken. Brad's face was the epitome of confusion, Jonathan's eyes a window to the rapid fire thoughts racing through his mind.

"Oh my God, it makes sense," Jonathan said. "Sophie was talking about Merlin just this morning. She said the reason he came to Mackinac was because it was the best of both worlds."

"Both worlds?" Mitch asked quickly.

"Yeah, a place to tell the news he loved, and a place that allowed him to escape his family."

Mitch tightened his hand into a fist and raised it in the air.

"We got him."

Twenty-Six
4:00 p.m.

ELISE LOOKED AT the picture in her hand once again, felt her heart twist at the sight of the family she loved so much.

"Sophie, I've got to go see Uncle Ken. Gotta make sure he's okay."

The woman nodded. "I know, hon. But it's almost dark out there. It's too dangerous."

Elise squeezed the woman's hand, forced the corners of her mouth upward in some semblance of reassurance. "I'll be fine. I'm a good skier. Pretty fast, too. I need to do this."

Sophie stood. "Then let me pour some hot cocoa in a thermos for you while you get yourself bundled up."

Elise watched Sophie push through the swinging doors into the kitchen, then looked back at the picture in her hand.

Oh, Uncle Ken. I know you loved them.

Sophie reappeared just moments later, a tall green thermos in her hands.

"I attached this strap to the thermos so you can sling it over your head and across your shoulder. It's what I do when I..."

Elise waited for the woman to continue, but she didn't.

"Thanks, Sophie." She knotted her scarf around her throat and pulled her insulated gloves above her wrists.

"What do I tell Mitch if he comes looking for you?"

"That I went back to the hotel to take a nap. He'll buy that with the poor sleep we got last night." Elise turned toward the door, her gaze falling on the undeveloped roll of film atop Sophie's counter. "Sophie, would you mind if I take that roll with me?"

"Not at all."

Twenty-Seven
4:25 p.m.

She was a good skier. Fast. Better than he was. But he could catch her if he wanted to.

Completing his list had given him a burst of energy like he'd never known before.

Sure, he would have liked his dad to be the last one. The cherry on the sundae, so to speak. But that was impossible. He needed to take care of the last two people who could identify him.

Jonathan would have to wait 'til later, when he was alone in his hotel room without the other cops around. But Elise—she'd made it easy when she left Sophie's and headed away from the police station.

Unfortunately, he was curious now. What would make a young woman head off into the woods alone? Especially when she knew he was out there somewhere.

Twenty-Eight
5:25 p.m.

ELISE STARED AT the flames in front of her, waited for their warmth to chase away the chill that permeated her entire body.

"You took quite a chance coming out here at this time of the day." Uncle Ken slipped a long brown afghan around her shoulders and gave her back a quick rub.

"I had to." Her voice sounded raspy, tired.

"What's wrong?"

She slipped her hand into the right front pocket of her jeans, closed her fingers around the photograph Sophie had given her. It was hard to reconcile what was right. Her head knew that showing the photograph to Uncle Ken might be a bad idea. But her heart longed to see the look on his face.

"Elise?"

Slowly, she pulled her hand from her pocket, the photograph cutting into her fingers.

"What do you have there?"

Wordlessly, she held the picture out, waited for him to take it from her hand.

She felt his questioning eyes on her face as he reached for the photograph and held it into the lantern light.

Elise saw Uncle Ken's eyes widen, his lips part.

"Where did you get this?" he asked, his voice suddenly hoarse.

"A woman in town had it. She figured out that I was the girl in the picture."

Uncle Ken raised his right hand to his cheek, his eyes never leaving the photograph. "Oh, how I miss them."

Elise reached out, grasped his empty hand with her own.

"I know you do. I do, too. But Ray is still out there. Somewhere."

Uncle Ken's entire demeanor changed, he pushed the photograph back into her hand and walked across the room. "Little Ray is better off without me in his life. To lose his father to cancer, and his mother to my stupidity? That's more than any person should have to bear."

She opened her mouth to argue, but stopped. The pain in Uncle Ken's eyes was so intense, so raw. It was a pain she couldn't wipe away in mere minutes. Or even days.

She turned to the fire once more. The flames crackled and popped as they danced on the log pile.

"I guess my afternoon angel isn't coming today."

"Afternoon angel?"

Uncle Ken nodded, pointed to a small framed photograph on a shelf beside the fireplace. A photograph she hadn't noticed during her first visit.

"That's Sophie!"

"She's been a lifeline for me these past few years." Uncle Ken walked over to the shelf and picked up the photograph. "I would have given up on life long before now if it weren't for her goodness and quiet understanding."

Realizing her uncle was speaking as much to himself as he was to her, Elise stood perfectly still. Listened.

"I'm not sure why, but she's made it her mission to be my contact with the outside world for the past twelve years." He stared at the picture as he continued. "Nearly everyday she arrives here around two-thirty and chats about this, that, or the other. Even on days when I've not said a word the entire time."

"So *you're* why she shuts her restaurant down everyday from two 'til four?" Elise asked.

Uncle Ken nodded, quietly placed the frame back on the shelf. "Faye would have liked her."

"Yes, she would have." Elise said quietly. "I like her, too. Though I've been a bit worried about her these past few days."

"Worried? Why?"

Elise bit back the excitement she felt at his obvious concern.

"She seems to get confused at times. I've been hoping it's just stress."

"Confused how?"

Elise pulled the afghan more closely around her shoulders and stepped away from the fire.

"Like today. I was at the restaurant with Jonathan."

"Jonathan? I thought your young man's name was Mitch."

"It is. Mitch went to question someone with Brad, while Jonathan and I stayed at Sophie's." Elise sat on the battered sofa in front of the hearth and pulled her legs up underneath her. "Jonathan is a retired police officer from Georgia. He's been helping in the investigation and we're very lucky to have him."

Her uncle nodded, his left eyebrow slightly cocked as he waited for her to continue.

"Anyway, I said something about Jonathan being a police officer and Sophie was surprised by that."

Elise stared at the fire as she continued. "Then she made a comment about how lucky we are to have four police officers on the island at a time like this."

Uncle Ken sat on the edge of a nearby recliner. "And?"

"I corrected her, pointed out there's just three. Mitch, Brad, and Jonathan," Elise said. "But she insisted there was another. One that she thinks was with Mitch and me that first night."

"Is there?"

Elise shook her head. "No. In fact, other than one very cold stranger, Mitch and I were the only ones in the restaurant that first night."

"Does she have a picture of this man she thinks is a cop?"

She stuck her hand into her left pocket and pulled out Sophie's roll of undeveloped film. "I'm hoping it's on here."

She studied her uncle, saw the way he looked at her with a twinkle in his eye. A twinkle she hadn't seen in years. "And you want to develop it now, right?"

"I thought you'd never ask. But is it even possible without some sort of light?"

"Does your watch have a light?" Uncle Ken asked.

Elise stared down at her wrist, at the watch that her grandfather had given her when she graduated from college. "Yes, it does. Why?"

"That's all we need."

IT HAD TAKEN five days, but they finally knew who the killer was. Even knew what he looked like. But now they needed to find him.

"Read that letter again. Doesn't it seem as if his father would be the last person on his list?"

Brad's question hung in the air, the first coherent thing he'd uttered in hours.

Mitch scanned the article in his hand once again, then studied the photograph on the desk in front of him. Brad's question made sense. Perhaps the killer was done.

"Maybe. Maybe he feels a sense of freedom now that the people who he feels wronged him are gone." Mitch stared into the eyes of the killer, waited to see if they'd speak to him somehow.

"Maybe. But he's got to know he isn't out of the woods yet," Jonathan said.

Mitch looked up from the photograph, the meaning behind Jonathan's words crystal clear.

"Why? Because we know who he is?"

He heard Brad's question, saw Jonathan's slow nod. But suddenly none of it meant anything to him. He knew the answer Brad was seeking. And it was an answer he didn't like.

"He doesn't know we can ID him. But he knows *someone* can." He ran his hand across his eyes and over his hair, felt the sudden moisture in his palms.

174

"Who?" Brad asked.

Mitch jumped to his feet and grabbed his parka.

"Elise!"

MITCH PUSHED SOPHIE'S door open and yelled, the panic in his voice obvious to his own ears.

"Sophie? Elise?"

The door to the back room swung open and Sophie emerged, drying her hands on a dish towel.

"Good heavens, Mitch? What's the matter?"

"Where's Elise?"

"Uh, she went back to—"

"We need the truth, Sophie," Jonathan said quietly. "Even if you promised."

Mitch stopped and looked back at Jonathan. "What are you talking about?"

"Is she in danger?" Sophie's quiet voice permeated the room, made Mitch turn once again to look into her eyes.

"She might be. Where is she?"

Sophie looked past Mitch, her eyes focused on the doorway. On Jonathan.

"Sophie? Jonathan? What's going on?"

Jonathan shut the door and ventured further into the tiny restaurant. He looked past Mitch, spoke directly to Sophie.

"Is she with him?"

Mitch stared at Jonathan, his hands growing moist inside his gloves. *"With who?"*

Sophie's hand grasped his forearm. "Elise is with her uncle. At his cabin."

"Her uncle? What uncle?"

Sophie gently guided Mitch into a chair and sat beside him. "Do you remember how she told you about visiting here with her aunt and uncle? How her aunt had died in an accident and she lost touch with her uncle after that?"

"Yeah."

"Well, he came back here. He's been here ever since."

Mitch pulled off his gloves and wiped his hands on his pants. "Why didn't she tell me when we planned this trip? Why was it a secret?"

Jonathan joined them. "She didn't know he was here. Until a few days ago when Brad apparently mentioned his name."

Mitch turned his attention to Brad. "You knew?"

Brad shook his head, his mouth open. "I didn't know. I have no clue what they're talking about right now."

Mitch pointed at Jonathan. "And you?"

"Just found out this morning."

"Who is this guy?"

Sophie sighed. "His name is Ken Fogarty."

Brad gasped. "Old man Fogarty? The freaky hermit?"

"He's not a hermit. And he's not a freak." Sophie's voice, strong and angry, filled the room. "He is a kind, gentle man who has been saddled with more guilt and grief than anyone should have to bear."

Mitch waited for the words he was hearing to make sense. But they didn't.

"I don't get this, Sophie."

"Elise's uncle married a woman about a year before they vacationed here. They had a wonderful marriage. It was a first for Ken. The second for Faye, who had a son. Her first husband died of cancer. Ken was a second chance at love for her, a second chance at a loving father for her son."

Mitch dropped his head into his palms and listened to Sophie tell him things about Elise that *he* should have known. Not Sophie.

"Two years later, she died of carbon monoxide poisoning. Ken had forgotten to turn his hotrod off when he left for work."

"Whoa." Mitch looked up. His heart twisted for this man he didn't know, a man who had to carry the burden of a loved one's death.

"I know, it must have been awful," Sophie said. "Apparently Elise's family turned against him. Faye's family turned against him—even going so far as to get custody of Faye's young son, Ray."

Mitch considered Sophie's words, waited for her to continue.

"Ken was so broken hearted that he retreated from the world. Came here. To the one place that brought him peace and made him feel connected to happier times."

"If Elise realized this on Thursday, why didn't she say something sooner?"

"She was worried about you and how her uncle's freedom might affect your feelings for her," Jonathan said.

"Affect my feelings for her? How? Why?" Mitch laid his head on the table, his heart heavy. "Wait. You don't have to answer that. She thought I would project my feelings for my father's killer onto her uncle?"

Sophie's confirmation came in the form of her soft fingers on his hand.

"And that's where she is now?" he asked quietly, his mind trying to grasp everything he'd just been told.

"Yes. She wanted to make sure he was okay. She's been terribly worried about him with this sicko on the loose."

Mitch pushed back his chair and stood.

"We've gotta get to her. Before the killer does."

Twenty-Nine
6:15 p.m.

EVER SINCE SHE was a little girl, Elise had always loved being in the darkroom with Uncle Ken. The idea of dipping an empty piece of paper into a "bath" had always made her giggle, the appearance of the final picture akin to pulling a bunny out of a hat.

Elise had certainly learned a few darkroom tips during those years, but never had she realized a watch light would be enough to develop a picture in an otherwise pitch-black room.

"You've learned a lot about darkrooms since I saw you last," Uncle Ken said over her shoulder.

"I have. Most of it was from you, stuff I still remember. But some of it is from the photographer at my paper. Dean. He's a little off-color, but you'd like him."

"I would have thought that most photographers today would be shooting with digital cameras."

Elise shook her head. "Not Dean. He wants total control over his camera, his pictures."

The room grew silent as she pushed the paper around in the fixer solution and waited for the pictures to appear.

"There you go." Uncle Ken's voice drew her attention from a past full of memories and onto the paper in front of her.

The first few images to appear were of smiling tourists, people who must have arrived in the twenty-four hour time period before her and Mitch.

"Everyone looks so happy," she said.

"It's a happy place."

She couldn't miss the wistful tone in her uncle's expression. It was obvious he was remembering their vacation to the island all those years ago.

She looked at the paper in front of her, at Mitch's smiling face, his arm wrapped around her protectively, lovingly.

"He looks like a nice guy."

"He's the best." She looked at Mitch's image, felt the longing to be with him. Here. "I think you two would hit it off, if you'd only give each other a chance."

A pounding sound made them both jump. She looked quickly at her uncle.

"I can't, Elise. I just can't."

"I'll get it, then." Elise opened the door of the darkroom and headed toward the front door, the still-wet photograph from that first night clutched in her hand.

As she strode across the family room, she looked down at the picture. Saw Mitch's smiling face, saw the restrained sparkle in her own eyes as she'd tried to push off thoughts of her uncle in favor of a relaxing vacation. And she saw Merlin at the table behind them.

Merlin?

She stopped in her tracks, stared at the editor's face partially hidden by the tightly drawn hood and the hint of brown hair that escaped.

Brown hair?

Confused, she looked at the picture more closely. Searched it for something that would make sense. But there was nothing.

The man at the table behind them was the same man who'd been covered in snow. The same man who'd sent a chill down her spine. And he was the same man she'd spent two days with, searching for something that would help them identify a killer.

But what about the hair? Could it be a brother?

The question was barely in her thoughts before the answer hit her like a ton of bricks. It was what had teased at her subconscious since the night they found Annie.

The basket of personal care items next to the walkie talkie at the Lakeside Inn. It had been short a bottle of shaving cream. She covered her mouth with her hand as the enormity of her thoughts hit her full force.

All of a sudden it made perfect sense why there hadn't been anything about the serial killer in the wire stories. He'd gotten rid of them. She'd just been too stupid to put two and two together. Until now.

Bits and pieces of their time together filtered through her thoughts. The way he hadn't known where the wire stories were kept. He'd explained it away on his illness, but that wasn't true. He'd opened up the wrong cabinet because he hadn't known.

The sloppy desk had bothered her the second time and now she knew why. Someone that sloppy wouldn't have had wire stories neatly arranged in a basket. He must have done that during the night, weeding out the ones he hadn't wanted her to read.

Her mouth dropped open as his words filled her ears.

"When I think of Annie, my head hurts. She was such a fighter."

A fighter.

Mitch and Brad had been certain Annie had fought with her attacker, the turned-over trash can and scattered pens indicative of a struggle. She'd fought him.

The pounding at the door continued. Without thinking, Elise unlocked the door and turned the knob. As she pulled the door open, she felt her stomach drop, her heart lurch.

Merlin.

"Surprised to see me?" The man's voice was oddly different, the endearing grumpiness she'd come to know, replaced by a chilling tone. She stared into the face of the man she'd put so much trust into, the face of the man who had taken the lives of Pete, Annie, and a man who was obviously the real editor of the paper, and suddenly knew exactly what she needed to do.

"Merlin! I thought you were dead!" Drawing on every ounce of courage and hope she had, Elise wrapped her arms around the man's neck and prayed her acting ability would pass as sincere. "It is so good to see you."

The man stood motionless for a moment, then stepped back, stared at her with an unreadable expression as she continued.

"Come in. You look cold. Why don't you sit right here and let me get you a blanket." Without waiting for a response, she reached for the afghan she'd used such a short time ago, and handed it to him. "Where have you been since the fire?"

As soon as the question left her mouth, she wished she could recall it. A question like that left him with only two options. To gamble with a believable answer, or admit the truth. The latter choice being a sure death sentence for her and Uncle Ken.

Uncle Ken!

She looked quickly at the closed door to the darkroom, knew her uncle was on the other side, terrified to come out, terrified to be with another human being. Afraid of judgment.

"Is someone in there, Elise?"

She swung her gaze back to Merlin, considered lying, but knew it was futile.

"My uncle's working in the darkroom. Would you like to meet him?"

Merlin jumped to his feet, his breath hot on her neck as he followed her to the doorway. "Yes. I would."

Uncle Ken emerged from the room, his eyes hooded and distant.

"Uncle Ken, this is Merlin Webber. He's editor of the paper here." Elise spoke softly, her feet still moving slowly toward the darkroom as she discreetly handed the newly-developed picture to her uncle.

"How long have you lived here?" Merlin's question surprised her, and she listened for Uncle Ken's answer as she made her way into the darkroom.

"Almost thirteen years."

The second the words were out of her uncle's mouth, she realized what they'd mean to a killer who didn't know about his secluded lifestyle. That kind of time on the island would mean that Ken would *know* he wasn't the editor.

MITCH SAW THE candlelit windows as soon as they rounded the last cropping of trees. It was the same cabin he'd pointed out to Elise from the sled that first afternoon.

Looking back, he could see the instances that had brought Elise pain, the times she'd grown quiet. He recalled how her hand had lingered on the red pushpin that represented this cabin. The way she'd snapped her pencil when Brad mentioned her uncle's name that first night. The way she'd insisted on going with the ski group to round up the outlying residents.

It all made sense now. Elise hadn't grown quiet because of a problem between them. She'd retreated because of the memories the cabin and the island had brought back. Memories she'd kept to herself, rather than share with him.

He shook his head and forced himself to focus on the cabin in front of him. Now was not the time to question the strength of their relationship.

"That's it." Brad pointed at the cabin with his ski pole.

Mitch pushed off the snow with his poles, took the lead as they approached the cabin.

"Mitch, wait. Let me go around back, in case something happens."

Mitch nodded at Brad, watched his buddy ski around the back of the small log home before continuing on his own path once again.

When he reached the front porch, Mitch bent down, unsnapped the straps that held his boots in place.

All was quiet from out here. But he knew that didn't mean a damn thing. Death was quiet.

Mitch stepped onto the porch and crept over to the door. He strained to hear noises on the other side but heard nothing.

Pulling off his gloves, he clenched and unclenched his hands in an effort to bring some feeling back to his fingers. He counted to three and reached for the doorknob, slowly turned it to the right. The door pushed inward an inch and he peered inside.

A bearded man standing to the left of an inner doorway met Mitch's eyes briefly, jerked his head toward the small room beyond where he stood.

Elise's uncle. It had to be.

Mitch met the man's eyes again, prayed he would understand the non-verbal question in his face. His stomach lurched when the man nodded in response.

Mitch quietly unzipped his parka, reached his hand toward his holster and closed his hand around his gun.

"I was trying to develop a roll of film when you knocked. I just need to finish that up." Elise walked into the darkroom, willed her voice to remain calm. "But we need to shut the door for it to be dark enough."

She prayed Uncle Ken would look at the picture she'd handed him, realize the man in the background was the one in his home now. Prayed he would leave his personal jail and venture out. For help.

Merlin was standing so close she could feel his breath on her neck as she shut the door, her eyes desperately trying to adjust to the lack of light.

Pressing the tiny button on the side of her watch, she held her arm to the countertop and the bottle of fixer she'd been using just moments earlier. Elise closed her left hand around the bottle, unscrewed the cap with her right.

"Merlin?"

"Yes."

"This is for Annie."

With one quick movement of her arm, she shot the open bottle forward, the liquid spattering in the man's face and eyes.

Elise heard the thud of his body as he fell backward against the wall, heard the high pitched screams as his eyes began to burn.

The door of the darkroom flung open and she looked up, saw Mitch's tall form standing in the doorway, his han wrapped around the grip of his gun.

"I got him, Mitch. I got him!"

She stared down at the wounded man huddled in the corner beside the open door. A man she had trusted.

"He killed Pete and Annie. And the real Merlin." Her voice cracked as she looked up at Mitch. "He killed them all."

Mitch's arms reached for her, pulled her close. "But you stopped him before he could hurt anyone else."

Thirty
9:00 p.m.

She felt Mitch's arms around her, felt the love he had for her. But there was something else there now. Something she hadn't felt before.

She knew what it was. It was apprehension. Maybe even a little mistrust.

"I'm sorry I didn't tell you about Uncle Ken sooner. I was afraid it would make you run."

She felt his warm lips against her forehead, his breath on her hair.

"Why would you think that?"

"I know how much pain your dad's murderer caused both you and your mom. I know how angry it makes you when people don't pay for their crimes. I guess I assumed you'd think my uncle should have been punished for Faye's death. Everyone else did."

"Forgetting to shut off a car is quite different than raising a gun and pulling the trigger," Mitch said softly.

She knew he was right. Felt it with every fiber of her being.

"I'm sorry, Mitch."

"I know."

Elise looked at the doorway that led to the darkroom, closed her eyes against the image of the killer that instantly filled her mind.

"So he really didn't kill Pete?"

Mitch shook his head slowly. "Nope. Josh Cummings murdered Pete. So *he* could win the competition and the prize money."

"Only he didn't win. Mark did."

Mitch rubbed his hand across his face. "Sad, isn't it?"

She stared at the fire in the hearth, watched the flames shoot upward toward the chimney.

"It makes sense. Now." She could hear the raspy sound to her voice as she continued. "When I think back to the first time we talked, Merlin seemed more shocked by the fact that there'd been *two* murders than he was by the actual crime itself."

"I'm sure he was thrown off by the fact that he wasn't the only killer on the island." Mitch touched his lips to her head and kissed her softly.

"But..."

"What?"

"It must have been horrible for Merlin's father to hear Jonathan and me in that office and not yell for help." Elise sat forward, met Mitch's eyes with her own. "Do you think he was gagged?"

Mitch took her hand in his. "We think he was dead before you ever showed up."

She stared at Mitch, waited for him to continue.

"Think about it, Lise. He took on the vocation of his victims. That says to me that Merlin must have been dead when you showed up the first time. Certainly by the second."

Elise looked at the fire for a moment as she pondered Mitch's words. It made sense. He took his father's career *after* he killed him.

"Do you think his last victim had been a cop?"

"Yeah. It would explain the intensity and loathing in the agent's voice that first night. And it jibes with what Joe told us during the sleigh ride that first day about the cop he brought into town after the noon flight."

"And it backs up why Sophie thought there were four cops," Elise said quietly as she looked down at her hands. "I'm so glad this is over, Mitch."

"Me, too."

She reveled in the feel of his warm hands as she peered at her uncle in the kitchen.

He'd responded well to Mitch. Even helped Brad and Mitch tie the killer up and get him onto the sled he had in his shed.

"Your uncle seems like a nice guy. It's a shame he's punished himself so much."

She swung her gaze back to Mitch. "It is. He loved Aunt Faye with his whole heart. He was an incredible stepfather to her son." She held her hand against Mitch's, entwined her fingers with his. "He made a mistake. That's all."

Uncle Ken walked into the sitting room, carrying a tray with three coffee mugs and some white napkins.

White.

"Uncle Ken? Was the guy you saw outside your cabin last Thursday the killer?" She reached for a mug of coffee and handed it to Mitch, waited for her uncle to answer.

"He was quite a distance off and his face was shadowed by the trees, but I'd say no. My guy was younger."

"Who are you talking about?"

Elise looked at Mitch. "I think my uncle saw the kid from the livery staring up at the cabin on the day we arrived."

Mitch took a quick sip of coffee. "Do you remember anything else?"

"He dropped something white. But that was five days and two feet of snow ago." Uncle Ken perched on the edge of the armchair.

"Something white?" Mitch asked.

"Yeah. Maybe paper of some sort."

"I wonder if it was R.J.'s letter."

"What letter?" Elise asked.

"Remember he told me he had a letter to give to someone?"

"Oh, then I'm sure it wasn't the same person. I don't have visitors." Uncle Ken cleared his throat and grabbed his own coffee mug from the tray. "So, this guy that Elise took out with the fixer, he didn't kill all three of the victims?"

Mitch shook his head. "Nope. He killed the desk clerk at the Lakeside Inn, and his father. The skier that was killed was the victim of a man who was desperate for a way to pay his divorce attorney."

Elise recalled the things the killer had said the day they met. Things that had seemed innocent at the time.

"Don't let your guard down around this red haired guy you told me about. Just in case your Mitch is right. Someone had to have killed that skier."

"Can you imagine the instant when he first realized he wasn't the only killer?" Elise leaned her head against Mitch's strong chest.

"I suspect he learned a whole lot standing outside Brad's open window." Mitch nuzzled his stubbly chin against the back of her head. "I'm sure he was well aware of the skier's disappearance thanks to our conversations. But yeah, I imagine he was elated when he realized Pete was dead. Took total focus off him."

"I guess that's how he knew about the fortuneteller murders and the article I had written, too. He heard Brad talking about it that first night, didn't he?"

Mitch nodded.

Elise saw her uncle frown down at his hands.

"Uncle Ken? You okay?"

The man shrugged. "It's just a shame that people can't find other ways to change their lives."

A quiet knock on the back door brought an end to the conversation.

"That would be my afternoon angel." He looked down at his wrist, then back at the door. "Making her very first evening call."

Elise watched the way her uncle's demeanor changed as he headed for the back door. Sophie brought a lift to his shoulders, a spring to his step.

He unlatched the back door and opened it, reached for Sophie's hand.

Elise smiled as Sophie walked through the door, followed closely by Mark and a young man with dark hair.

"Hey there Mark, R.J. What are you guys doing here?" Mitch kissed Elise's head quickly, then rose to his feet and walked toward the door.

"We made a connection that we thought some of you might be interested in," Sophie said, a smile spreading across her face.

Elise stared at the young man who reached for Mitch's outstretched hand. She recognized the ocean-blue eyes that sparkled as he smiled.

"Ray?" Elise's voice was echoed by Uncle Ken's as she, too, rose to her feet.

"Elise?"

Relief flooded through her body, happiness filled her heart. She looked at Uncle Ken, saw the disbelief in his eyes as he stood transfixed in the same spot he'd been when Ray walked through the door.

She ran around the sofa, wrapped her arms around the young man's shoulders and held him close. "Oh, Ray, we've missed you so much."

"I've missed you, too, Elise." He held her closely for several moments and then stepped back, reached for Uncle Ken's hand. "I've missed you, too, Ken."

Uncle Ken cleared his throat, too shocked to speak.

"Before you say a word, Ken, I need you to know something. I need you to know you didn't do anything wrong that morning."

Elise stared at Ray, her heart pounding.

"I did, son. I was careless. And there's not a day that's gone by that I haven't regretted my stupidity or wished it had been me instead of your mom."

Ray pulled a piece of folded paper from his pocket and held it outward. "I lost the envelope out by your shed a few days ago. But it doesn't matter. What matters is that it wasn't an accident. *Mom* left that car running. She was trying to keep us from watching her die a slow, painful death."

Elise sucked in her breath, waited for Ray to continue or for Uncle Ken to respond.

Ken reached for the letter, unfolded it, and read.

189

Moments later, his shoulders sagged and he began to cry. A quiet, heartbreaking cry that made her heart ache with pain. And love.

"Ray, how long have you known this?" Elise asked quietly.

"I just found out. I came across the letter in a journal my mom kept. I think she assumed someone would find it after she died."

Uncle Ken wiped the tears from his face, held a hand over his mouth momentarily. "It makes sense now. She had a lot of appointments that last year. When I questioned her about them, she'd say they were routine. But she'd grown so pale back then. You can even see it in this picture." He picked up the picture Elise had shown him and stared down at it.

"But why would she take her own life?" Elise asked quietly.

It was Uncle Ken that answered. "Because she didn't want Ray to suffer through the sickness of another parent. Don't you see? She didn't intend for all of this to happen. She was trying to do what she thought was best."

Elise felt Mitch's eyes watching her closely, was grateful for the feel of his arm on her shoulders.

"Now you know. Now you can live again," Sophie said quietly as she rested her head on Ken's shoulder.

Tuesday, February 1st
Thirty-One
12:30 p.m.

ELISE SAT IN front of Sophie's laptop, determined to bring closure to a week of hell. Determined to preserve a part of island history that the real Merlin would have wanted.

The F.B.I. had made it onto the island earlier that morning, pockets of power and phone service had been restored overnight. Merlin's son had been cuffed and taken away, Josh removed from Jonathan's watch with the promise of jail time.

The federal agents had even allowed everyone to call home, tell their loved ones and co-workers that they were okay.

She smiled as she remembered Dean's words.

"Lise, what did I tell you? Everything comes back to a picture. Once again, it was a photograph that helped catch a killer. Photography is the heart and soul of everything. Reporters are becoming obsolete."

She looked across the restaurant at Uncle Ken. Just seeing him outside his cabin, in the company of other people was encouraging. Watching the sparkle in his eyes as he sat between Sophie and Ray was a dream come true. He looked so happy and at peace. Ready to face a world that had judged him unfairly. Ready to share his home with Ray.

And Sophie—she was a special lady. The kind of woman she'd love to have for an aunt one day.

Elise swiped at the tear that escaped her eye as she saw Ray's arm drape across the back of Uncle Ken's chair. The horrible nightmare that had kicked off their vacation was over.

In its place was hope. Hope for Uncle Ken. Hope for Ray. Hope for her relationship with Mitch.

Her eyes instinctively moved to Mitch's table, watched him laughing and joking with Brad and Jonathan. Even Mark seemed at ease as he listened to the guys recount the happenings of the past few days.

They were good guys. All of them.

Elise studied Brad as he leaned back in his chair, his foot curled precariously around the leg of the table. As hard as it was to watch someone give up a dream, Brad's decision to get out of police work was probably a good idea. He had a big heart and was a nice guy, but he needed more than that to be a cop. She just wasn't sure if the island really needed another fudge shop. But time would tell.

Jonathan was one of those people you count your blessings for having met. Solid, loyal, honest. The kind of qualities she imagined Mitch's late father having.

She watched as Jonathan rested a hand on Mitch's shoulder as they traded stories, saw the respect and admiration in Mitch's face. There was no doubt about it, the two men had formed a bond over the past few days. A bond that wouldn't end because one lived in New Jersey, the other in Georgia. In fact, Jonathan was already talking about a summer vacation to Ocean Point.

Smiling, Elise scanned the wall next to her small table, her eyes coming to rest on the picture Sophie had tacked up that morning. A picture of Elise with Uncle Ken, Ray, and Mitch. Her family. Her loved ones.

She looked back at Mitch, met his sparkling eyes across the room. Her heart jumped as he pushed back his chair and walked over to the table where she sat.

"Having trouble writing?"

"No. Maybe. A little. There's just so many thoughts swirling through my head right now."

"Enough to write a book?"

She felt the corners of her mouth turn upward, heard the laugh escape her lips.

"Oh no. No way. Not another Madame Mariah prediction. I think this *eventful* vacation was enough, don't you?"

Mitch shrugged. "Maybe. But what harm can come from writing a book? You're certainly good enough."

She reached up and gently guided his head downward until their lips were just inches apart. "Thank you."

"You're welcome."

"I'm sorry I didn't tell you about Uncle Ken from the start." She searched his face for forgiveness.

"It's okay. I understand. You were trying to protect what we have. But you don't need to do that. I'm in this for the long haul. And nothing anyone else does can change my feelings for you. Got it?"

"Got it."

Her stomach jumped as his lips met hers and lingered ever so softly. Never in her wildest dreams could she have imagined finding a man like Mitch.

He ran his hand gently down her cheek, brushed a wayward curl from her face. "Now get back to writing so we can salvage what's left of this vacation before we have to head back to Jersey."

"Can we cuddle by the fire?"

"Oh yeah."

"Can we ski together?"

"Yup. And you don't even have to teach me. I'm a self-taught wonder."

She laughed.

"Can we spend some time with Uncle Ken and Ray, I mean, R.J.?"

"Definitely." He ran his lips across her forehead. "Besides, I've got something I want to ask you while we're here. With them."

"Ask me?"

"Ask you." Mitch cleared his throat as a nervous look flickered in his eyes. "I just pray you say yes."

She stared at him as he winked and walked away.

Could he mean what she thought he meant?

Finally she had the incentive she needed to get her article written. Positioning her hands on the keyboard in front of her, she began to write:

As the clouds rolled in, weather forecasters in the Mackinac Island area predicted the impending arrival of a massive blizzard—a storm that would likely leave island residents stranded without power, phones, and access to the mainland.

But that was only the beginning of a forecast far more menacing than the meteorologists could imagine. This unforgettable blizzard blew in more than just deep snow and howling winds. It brought with it the promise of evil like this island has never seen. An evil that did not win...

Laura Bradford was bitten by the writing bug at the tender age of ten. But instead of being a fleeting childhood phase, the desire to write grew into a career that has included journalism, business writing, short fiction, and finally novels. She attributes much of her success to the people who believed in her ability along the way—teachers, Girl Scout leaders, her first editor, and a treasured friend.

Her nearly lifelong love affair with the mystery genre was sparked by a handful of Nancy Drew books and ignited by her all-time favorite author, Mary Higgins Clark.

The publication of Laura's debut novel, *Jury of One*, was the realization of a childhood dream, yet the beginning of a journey. A journey she hopes will be an inspiration to all children who dream of being a writer some day.

Since its release, *Jury of One* has gone on to be a book club selection for Harlequin's Worldwide Mysteries. Its sequel, *Forecast of Evil*, follows news reporter Elise Jenkins and Detective Mitch Burns on their long awaited vacation to a small Michigan island. A vacation complete with haunting family secrets and a faceless killer.

Laura lives in Missouri with her husband and two daughters. She is a member of both Sisters in Crime and Mystery Writers of America.

To learn more, visit her website: www.laurabradford.com

Printed in the United States
51518LVS00003B/211-225